The Cowboy and His Billionaire

Cowboys of Rock Springs, Texas #6

Kaci M. Rose

Five Little Roses Publishing

Book Cover By: **Sarah Kil Creative Studio**

Editing By: Debbe @ **On the Page, Author and PA Services**

Proofread By: Violet Rae

Dedication

To the coffee that kept me going and the kids
that call me mommy.

Blurb

He's a small town doctor. She's a big city CEO billionaire. Fate is about to show them they need each other, in and out of the office.

Kayla rolls into the small town of Rock Springs in her fancy suit and expensive high heels ready to do a business deal and then head back to Dallas.

Getting hurt and meeting Brice, the small-town cowboy doctor, wasn't part of the plan.

Neither was being stuck in town because she can't drive and the business deal failed.

Bryce went away to school, did the big city doctor thing, and hated every minute of it.

So he came home, took over his dad's practice with plans to settle down with a small-town girl.

That is, until Kayla is brought into his office unconscious.

One look at her and his whole world is turned upside down.

Now she's trying to find a way out of town as soon as possible and he's doing everything he can to get her to stay.

It's a battle of wills. May the best man or woman win.

Contents

Get Free Books!

Would you like some free cowboy books?
**If you join Kaci M. Rose's Newsletter you get
books and bonus epilogues free!**

**Join Kaci M. Rose's newsletter and get your
free books!**
https://www.kacirose.com/KMR-Newsletter

Now on to the story!

Chapter 1
Kayla

The city of Dallas grows smaller and smaller in my rearview mirror and I have no idea what to expect as I head toward the tiny town of Rock Springs, Texas.

I grew up in the city. My parents started a new multi-billion dollar company and as an only child, it was drilled into me that I would take over someday.

That someday was four months ago when my dad stepped down as CEO and became a board member, and I stepped up as CEO. I know many of the guys think I'm only in the position because of my dad, which is why I work twice as hard to prove to them I deserve to be there. But I know they're all waiting for me to fail.

Like my dad, I trust my gut and it's never let me down. I went all out in my presentation to the Board when I pitched the idea to franchise the little honky-tonk in the town of Rock Springs where an award-winning chef works. Surprisingly, the Board gave me the go-ahead. They want to see what happens.

Translation? They don't think it was a good idea and want to see me fall on my face.

"Take the next exit and turn right on County Road..."

My GPS informs me I'm finally at my exit and I move to the right side of the highway.

But Rock Springs isn't even listed on the exit sign. In Texas, that means the town is too tiny to even mention. Great.

After I take the exit, I start practicing my pitch for the owners. I know this is a good idea and I intend to prove the Board wrong. I can't let my first big acquisition as CEO be a flop. Even more importantly, I can't let my parents down. They've always done so much for me.

They're the kind of parents who, while running a huge company, were still at every ballet practice and performance. No matter what they had going on, they were always there and didn't miss a thing. They still managed to build this company together, and I won't let them down.

After miles and miles of cows and horses, I finally see signs of life, and the welcome sign lets me know I'm in the right place.

Welcome to Rock Springs, Texas.

Making the turn on Main Street, I slow down to take in the tiny town. There's a sign for a B&B on my right, and up ahead is WJ's where I'll be having my meeting. It's currently closed, and they have no idea I'm coming.

On my right is a small cafe which seems to be bustling with the entire population of the small town. I grab a parking spot and head inside to grab some coffee and kill time. I pull out my phone to check if I have service here, and the next thing I know a solid hunk of muscle barrels into me.

Before I even look up into his face, I know he's a cowboy because of the cowboy boots and

Wranglers he's wearing. If we were In Dallas, I'd tell him to watch where he was going and keep on walking. But I've done enough research to know that everyone in this town knows everyone, and I don't want to piss people off before I have Jason and Nick's signature.

So, pasting on a smile, I look up at the gentleman in front of me.

"You should get yourself a pair of boots. You'll break an ankle around here in those things," he says, nodding to my heels.

"Thanks, but I'm just in town to talk to the owners of WJ's." I point across the street. "Any idea when it opens?"

"Anytime now. Jason's wife cuts hair at the beauty salon. He likes to come in early with her so he might be down there," he says, pointing down the street behind me. "I'm happy to tell him you're looking for him, Miss...?"

"Kayla," I say, offering nothing more. My surname will reveal too much. It's better I'm only known as Ms. Bartrum right now.

"Well, the diner here has some good food while you're waiting," he suggests.

I shake my head as I look through the window next to us. "Thanks, but I'm here on business."

The diner is like something out of a movie. Everyone has turned in their chairs, not even trying to hide their curiosity as they watch us through the big picture window.

"Okay, city girl, you be careful." The man tips his hat at me and walks over to his truck.

Something about our interaction feels... off. Different. Like there's something I'm missing that I can't quite put my finger on. When he reaches his truck, he turns to look back at me and our eyes lock for just a moment before he nods at me and climbs behind the wheel.

Shaking it off, I take a deep breath and head into the diner. I'm greeted by silence and everyone is openly staring at me. The customers are all dressed in jeans, cowboy hats, and dusty boots, so I stick out like a sore thumb in my pencil skirt, heels, and silk blouse.

"Can I help you?" The woman behind the counter asks in a slow, southern Texan drawl.

"Umm, yes, a large coffee to go, please," I reply, walking over to the counter.

As I pay for my coffee, she turns to fill my order. "What brings you to Rock Springs?" she asks, and I can see everyone in the entire place watching intently.

"I have a meeting."

"It's never a good thing when city folk show up in town. The last one wanted to do something with resort condos."

"How do you know I'm a city girl?"

"The way you're dressed. No one around here dresses like that."

I cock an eyebrow at her.

"Maybe I dressed this way to purposely intimidate the other person?"

I know how this small-town works. The moment I'm out the door, everyone will be on their phones spreading the news, and I lose my upper hand. Tough. I don't like to lie, but it might be for the best.

"I have a meeting with a rancher outside of town. I'm just stopping for coffee to kill a bit of time."

"Mmm," she says, handing me my coffee, her tone letting me know she doesn't believe me.

"Thank you." I smile, and as I make my way out of the diner, I decide to have a bit of fun.

"When you all make your calls about me, be sure to mention that the shoes are Jimmy Choo, Give them the really juicy gossip." With that, I wink, then head out the door just as a truck pulls into WJ's parking lot.

Game time.

I get back in my car and check my makeup. It's still in place. Then I drink some coffee and reapply my lipstick before backing out of my parking space and driving over to WJ's. As I park, a second truck pulls in right behind me and a guy gets out. I recognize the guy from my research. It's Nick, the chef who won all the awards.

"We aren't open yet," he says, sounding mildly irritated as I step out of my car.

"I'm Kayla Bartrum. I'd like a moment to speak with you and Jason," I say holding out my hand.

Nick doesn't move. He just looks me up and down before nodding toward the door.

"It's only a handshake. I promise, I'm friendly," I smile.

"You'd better tread carefully. My wife would beat you down with those fancy Jimmy Choo's if you touch me."

Damn, news travels fast here–faster than I was expecting. At least he holds the door open for me as he gestures for me to follow him inside.

This is the first time I've been inside WJ's, but I've seen photos and videos of it online. Plus, earlier this month, I sent one of my employees to check the place out.

The place has an authentic Texan feel. There's a stage for live music and a dance floor. Worn wooden planks line the walls bearing the brand marks of local ranches. Wooden tables and chairs fill the space, and there's also an outdoor seating area as well. When WJ'sthey started serving Nick's food, the place became more family-friendly and began to make a name for itself. Which is why I think it's the perfect place to franchise out.

"Jason!" Nick calls as he enters the bar behind me.

The man standing at the bar–Jason, I assume–is huge. Behind him is an American flag made from red, white, and blue beer cans.

"Who's this?" Jason asks as I approach the bar with Nick.

"Kayla Bartrum," Nick replies, joining Jason behind the bar.

"We say no, so they send out some chick to seduce us? Save your time, sweetheart. We're both very happily married and not interested in *anything* you have to offer."

I take a deep breath. I wish I could say this is the first time someone has had this reaction but I'm aware that many companies employ the tactic of sending the hot girl to stroke a male ego or two to secure a potential business deal.

"I'm insulted that you think my company would do that. I'm the CEO, and I can assure you this is not a method we employ. If a company has to stoop that low, they don't deserve your business." I say, keeping my chin held high.

Jason and Nick glance at each other before returning their gazes at me.

"Then, why are you here?" Jason asks.

He's a bit taller than Nick, but they're both in Wranglers, flannel shirts, and sporting a five o'clock shadow. You know, the cowboy uniform.

"I believe in this idea, so at least let me give you my spiel before you kick me out," I say, stalling them as they open their mouths.

"Fine. You can talk as we set up the bar," Jason says.

I launch into my pitch, telling them how being a part of a franchise in Texas will benefit them. Nick will create all the signature recipes, and they'll have control over designs, as well as being the face of the company, while we provide the financial backing and split the profits. I lay it all out, complete with graphs, predictions, and marketing.

They let me talk and look over it all, but the moment I'm done they don't hesitate. "Our answer is still no. I'm sorry you wasted your time today," Jason says. Nick nods his head in agreement.

I cock my head. These two are hard to read. Usually, something in my presentation catches a client's interest but they couldn't have cared less.

"Can I ask what you don't like about my proposal?" If I know their objections, I have something to work with.

"We're small town folks," Nick says. "I could work in any restaurant in Dallas, but I stay here because of my family and the people."

"When I inherited this place it was just some hole in the wall," Jason adds. "Yeah, I've expanded it but it's still WJ's Rocks Springs. You want to take the personality out of it and mass produce it. You want to take it from a mom and pop place to a major chain. Look around this town. There's nothing here. No chains but the Dairy Queen."

"All this corporate stuff isn't for us. Let me walk you out," Nicks says.

"I'll take her. I need to go talk to Ella, anyway," Jason says. "She and Megan will be wanting the gossip as soon as this one leaves town."

"Tell Ella to pass it on to her sister so she isn't hounding me all day, too," Nick smirks.

They must read my confusion as I'm packing up my papers.

"Nick is married to Megan, who's my wife's sister," Jason says.

"Business partner and family. It really is like an old country song," I say as I turn to leave. "Thank you for your time. But I don't give up so easily."

"Don't suspect you do. It'll take a lot more than you've come up with to win us over." Jason opens the door for me.

I walk across the dirt and gravel parking lot and turn to tell Jason I'll talk to him soon when it all happens in slow motion.

As I turn, the rocks under my foot move and my heel catches. When I try to steady myself with my other foot, it ends up in a small pothole and twists. I hear a snap and my legs give out.

Jason can't get to me fast enough and a searing pain hits my temple as I fall. Then the world goes black.

Chapter 2

Brice

I hate stitches.

I swear the number of stitches I've administered lately is climbing by the day. Kids trying to do things they saw online but have no business doing themselves. On the flip side, stitches are easy to apply so the patient can get on their way. Well, on their way to being grounded and dealing with the parents.

Since I have a break in patients, I'm heading down to my parent's ranch and seeing how the new calf that was born last night is doing. Dad and I were up well past midnight with him and his momma, but they were both doing well when I left this morning.

I feel torn between both places. While I love being a doctor, I feel at home on the ranch, too. Growing up, I spent a lot of time on my best friend, Ford's, family ranch but I never thought of being a rancher until my dad retired and became one.

In order for my father to retire, I took over his doctor's practice. His version of retiring was to become a full-time rancher and pulling me in to help. I knew from an early age I wanted to be a doctor just like my dad, and I knew I wanted to do it here in Rock Springs where you can really get to know your patients. But like all small towns, the gossip flows just as freely in my waiting room as it does at the beauty salon.

I'm making notes on the last patient's file in my office when a commotion out front draws my attention.

I know my receptionist, Joy Miller, can handle anything. She started out with my dad and has seen it all in this town. But even though Joy knows everyone and is tough as nails, I'm a little concerned, so I step out and see what's happening.

I get one foot out of my office and even the normally calm Joy looks worried.

"Put her in here, Jason, and tell Brice what happened," Joy orders.

Jason is carrying the woman I bumped into at the coffee shop earlier. She's unconscious and has blood running down the side of her face.

"What the hell happened?" I ask, accessing her injuries while Jason gets her situated.

I did several rotations in big city emergency rooms, so I know all about staying calm under pressure, but something about seeing this girl like this unravels me, and I'm not sure why.

On top of the blood, there's dirt on her clothes and her ankle is starting to swell. From the looks of it, she took a nasty fall, which Jason confirms.

"She was leaving the bar and turned to say something to me, and the gravel just gave out under her feet. I couldn't move fast enough. One of her feet landed in a pothole and she fell, hitting her head on a rock. She hasn't woken up since. I brought her straight here."

"Joy, get her vitals." I start with the bump on her head where all the blood is and get it cleaned up.

"The workmen are coming tomorrow to level out the parking lot and this wouldn't have happened," Jason mumbles.

"If she was wearing the right shoes, it wouldn't have happened," I say, thinking of the conversation I had with her outside the diner.

After just a few minutes, I can tell the cut on her head is going to need a stitch or two, but she'll be ok. I gently remove her shoes to get a better look at her ankle. I'm pretty sure it's just sprained, but I want to x-ray it to be sure. I'll wrap it and she'll need to ice it, but she won't be wearing those fuck me heels anytime soon.

The town pitched in a few years back and got one of those portable x-ray machines like Hunter, the vet, uses because they hated the drive to go get one. I'm grateful more than ever to have it. I check the vitals Joy took, which all look good.

"After I get her head cleaned up, she'll need a few stitches for that gash. I'm pretty sure her ankle is just sprained but I'll x-ray it to be sure, though her vitals look good. Her name is Kayla, right?"

They don't need to know I ran into her earlier today. There's already been plenty of talk about her in the office today.

"Yes," Jason says.

Kayla begins to stir, and I step to her side in preparation for when she opens her eyes so I can check on her. Her eyes open but then she shuts them again with a groan.

"Joy, dim the lights," I instruct, then take Kayla's hand in mine.

As soon as the lights dim, she opens her eyes again and looks around. "Where am I?" she asks.

"You took a nasty fall in the parking lot, so I brought you to see the doctor," Jason explains.

"You have a doctor in this tiny town? Well, where is he?" She takes a deep breath, looking up at the ceiling.

"That would be Brice, here," Joy says.

Everyone calls me Brice. Very few people around here call me doctor because they all grew up with me. If I'm being honest, I like it that way.

"That would be me," I tell her.

"You're too young," she states as if I'm lying to her.

I don't even get to correct her before Joy comes to my defense.

"Brice was taking college courses while he was still in high school. Then he took summer classes and graduated early as head of his class. He's had job offers from Dallas to New York City but, thankfully, he wanted to come home and take over his dad's practice. You're lucky he did, or else you'd still be in the car on the way to the next closest doctor, young lady." Joy exaggerates a little, but I don't correct her.

"I'm sorry. I get pre-judged in my position all the time," Kayla apologizes. She looks over at Jason, and I wonder what he might have said to her earlier. "I shouldn't have done that to you."

I squeeze her hand and smile, "I'm used to it from those who aren't from around here."

She doesn't pull her hand away, so I continue to hold it. I'm not sure why I do, but there is this overwhelming need to have the connection to her.

"So, what's the damage doctor?" she asks.

No sooner do I open my mouth than there's more commotion in the waiting room

"Jason!" a female voice calls.

"I knew she'd come down here. Even though I told her not to," Jason mutters.

Joy opens the door and Ella, Jason's wife, bursts into the room. She heads right for Jason's arms and tucks herself into his side. Even though no one thought they would, those two just fit. He's older and a bar owner. She was raised in a strict church-going family, but somehow their worlds meshed.

"I told you I was fine and not to come down here," Jason says, kissing the top of her head.

"Yeah, but you wouldn't tell me if you were hurt until you got home, so I wasn't going to wait around."

I chuckle because it's true. I've treated Jason for some wounds from the bar, and every time he waits to tell Ella until he's patched up.

"Ella, this is Kayla," Jason says. "She's with the company from Dallas. When she took a spill in our parking lot, I brought her here."

"Just to be clear, I own the company in Dallas," Kayla says with sass, even though she's laying there on my exam table with a head wound

"Well, with those shoes, I'm surprised you lasted this long without taking a spill," Ella says.

"I told her that at the diner," I agree.

Kayla shoots me a glare, pulling her hand from mine.

"You'll need a few stitches and I'll clean up the cut on your temple. Your ankle needs an x-ray, but I'm pretty sure it's just a sprain. It will be several weeks before you can walk on it again."

I pull out the penlight I keep on me in the office and take a look at her eyes. "You also seem to have a mild concussion, so you need to be monitored for the next forty-eight to seventy hours. Let's get the bleeding stopped and cleaned up, then we'll get you an x-ray," I add.

"I'll clean her up if you want to walk them out," Joy says.

I nod, giving Kayla one last look before following Jason and Ella out to the waiting room. By the grace of God, there isn't a group of people here wanting the news straight from the source.

"You let me know how she is before she leaves. We'll cover any fees," Jason says.

"She's the one with money," I say. "How about we let her pay the fees?"

I know he doesn't like the idea, but he agrees.

"Come on, let Nick open the bar today, and let's go home and rest," Ella says, taking his hand.

"If I had a pretty lady like that trying to drag me home, I wouldn't hesitate," I say. "Go. I promise I'll text you with an update."

Jason finally gives in, and they leave. Standing there in the empty waiting room, I look down at my hand. I can still feel the warmth of her hand in mine. I swear I'm going crazy.

Shaking it off, I go back into the exam room and get everything I need to stitch her up. Joy did a great job cleaning the cut and after a little local numbing medicine, she's ready to go.

"You're lucky this is right at your hairline. There shouldn't be a scar, but if there is, no one will see it unless they get this close," I tell her.

"I think your idea of luck and mine are a little different," she chuckles.

"I'll go get the x-ray machine warmed up," Joy says, leaving the room.

"All done. Two switches and you're good to go—with that injury, anyway. Now for the X-ray. The Baron boys were in here last week and broke our wheelchair. Since I don't want you walking just yet, I'm asking your permission to carry you down the hall to the x-ray room."

The x-ray machine is portable but it's too bulky to bring into the exam rooms, so we keep it in its own room with an exam table.

"Do I have a choice?" Kayla asks.

"Well, you can refuse the x-ray but if it is broken and sets wrong, you won't be wearing those heels again. You may even end up with a slight limp."

Kayla curses under her breath and nods her head. "Fine, let's get this over with."

I scoop her up and she wraps her arms around my neck. Having her pressed up against me like this has my cock instantly hard. What the fuck? How inappropriate is this?

Carefully, I maneuver her down the hallway to the room with the x-ray machine and place her gently on the exam table. Thankfully, Joy has her back to us getting the machine setup so I can turn without anyone seeing me and adjust myself before moving on.

Once her x-rays are completed, I carry her back to the exam room she was in earlier. Though I might have been moving slower than I needed to just to enjoy having her in my arms a bit longer. If she realized, she didn't say a word.

I get her settled on the exam table. "I'm going to go read the x-rays and I'll be right back. Joy will be in to get you some water and anything else you need," I tell her and make a beeline for my office.

I can't remember the last time my cock was this hard or I wanted a woman in my arms so damn bad.

What the hell is wrong with me?

Chapter 3
Kayla

My head hurts, my ankle hurts, and my pride hurts.

What a great impression I must have made on Jason and Nick. If I thought I had an uphill battle to win them over before, it just got steeper.

Of course, I end up at the one office in the state of Texas which has a doctor who looks like he's just come off the set of some sexy soap opera. And what are the odds-a broken wheelchair? Though, I doubt any of the women around here would mind being carried around by him.

Resting my head on the exam table, I close my eyes. The light hurts my eyes more than I want to admit, and I know there's no way I'm getting home to Dallas tonight. I remember the sign for the bed-and-breakfast as I drove into town. I guess I'll try to get a room there. If I have to, I'm not above sleeping in my car.

The door opens but I don't open my eyes right away, knowing the hallway light is too bright.

"Oh, no, you don't. Wake up, Kayla." Brice's sexy deep voice fills the room as his hand lands on my shoulder.

Something about my name on his lips sends goosebumps racing across my skin. My name has never been said quite like that before, all gravelly and inviting. Slowly, I open my eyes and move my head to the side to look at him. He pulls up his rolling chair and sits next to me at eye level.

"Your x-ray confirms your ankle isn't broken. It's just a bad sprain. You're going to have to stay off it for a few weeks, ice it, and let it heal. Once you're using it again, your ankle won't be as steady due to the inactivity. After that, it will be a few months before you should even consider wearing heels again."

"Great," I sigh.

On the flip side, what girl doesn't love an excuse to go out and buy new shoes? I can build up a collection of flats to wear.

"Also, you have a mild concussion, so you need to take it easy. No driving back to Dallas right now."

"I planned to get a room at the bed-and-breakfast. Anyway, I don't feel like driving tonight."

"Unfortunately, that won't work. Someone needs to check on you over the next forty-eight hours, so it's best you aren't alone."

"Well, what do you suggest? I can't drive home, not that there's anyone there, anyway."

He sighs, looking at the floor, and swears under his breath.

"You can stay with me for a few days." He looks up and his eyes meet mine.

"No, I'll be fine at the bed-and-breakfast." Because my gut says staying in this man's house is a very, very bad idea. Even if the rest of my body wants to jump at the chance.

"Not an option." He shakes his head.

"Do you always offer to let patients stay with you?" I try to make my point.

"Only CEOs who can't currently walk, trying to sell out my friend's business.."

"I'm not trying to sell them out," I huff, causing him to chuckle. "I don't have any clothes, toiletries, and I have to get my car...." I start listing off my to-do list as my mind begins to whirl.

"Slow down. Joy already said Maggie, Nick's wife, is on her way in. She's bringing some clothes because Joy is certain you two are the same size. Then she'll follow Nick to my house and bring your car."

"Seems everything is planned out for me."

"It's what we do around here. What else do you need?"

"Assuming my purse made it here with me and my phone is still in it, nothing I can think of."

"All right, let's get you some crutches. Ever used them before?"

"Nope. But I'm sure they will match my work clothes perfectly."

"No need to be sarcastic. You're the one who wore high heels to a ranching town. Business meeting or not. You'd have more respect from them if you were in boots."

"Then I wouldn't have gotten to meet you," I sass back, and he just shakes his head again.

Before he can say anything, the door opens a crack.

"Maggie is on her way. If you have your keys, she'll stop here and grab them," Joy says.

"I guess they're in my purse."

Brice stands and grabs my purse from the counter, handing it to me. My keys are right on top and so is my cell phone. I resist the urge to check it and see what calls or texts I've missed. I'm not sure what to tell everyone just yet.

We spend the next twenty minutes getting me balanced on the crutches. Then Brice closes up the office.

"You don't have any more patients?" I ask.

"Nothing that couldn't be rescheduled."

"What about any other emergencies?"

He shrugs, locking the door behind me. "Believe it or not, they are few and far between. But most everyone here has my number. It's on the sign on the door and the office forwards it to my phone."

"No answering services?"

"No, City Girl. We're a bit more personable out here," he chuckles just as a truck pulls into the parking lot.

"So much for sneaking out early."

"That's just Maggie," Brice says, walking over to her.

Rolling down her window, Maggie says, "They weren't joking. She's pretty."

"I sure hope it wasn't Nick saying that," Brice says.

"You think I'd let him live if it was? No, Mrs. Willow called me, as did Abby, and even Savannah."

"News travels fast," I say.

"Well, it isn't often we have some big Dallas CEO here, much less one that gets hurt and stays at the Doc's house."

"Speaking of." Brice hands her my keys.

"I'll bring the stuff in when I get there," Maggie nods.

"My phone charger, too, please!"

"I'll get it! Don't you worry. See you two in a bit."

She circles around, leaving the parking lot. Brice helps me to his truck, takes the crutches from me, and makes sure I'm buckled in before going around to his side.

As we pull out of the parking lot, we pass the bed-and-breakfast. A minute later, we're back at the main road with WJ's to my left.

I pull out my phone. "Time to face the music."

It's filled with texts, missed calls, and emails. I ignore them all and call the most important one—my dad.

"How did the big meeting go?" My dad asks when he picks up, proving he was waiting for my call.

"Not great, but, um, I need to know how to handle something." I glance over at Brice who gives me a quick look before setting his eyes back on the road.

"Do I need to be in Dad mode or business mode?" This is how we've separated work and family since I started working with him and it's kept my mom sane, to say the least.

"Let's start with Dad mode. When I was leaving, I missed my step and fell. Twisted my ankle and hit my head. I'm fine. My ankle is sprained, and I can't walk on it. Unfortunately, I have a mild concussion and am unable to drive back to Dallas."

"Your mother and I'll be on the first flight out," he says.

"No, Dad, listen. I'm okay. Your meeting tomorrow is important and I'm not alone." I look at Brice who has just a hint of a smirk on his face. "But I wanted you to know. Now into business mode. I won't make it back to the office for a few days and I really don't want everyone there to go easy on me because I'm hurt. How do I handle it?"

Dad pauses for a moment and thinks it over. He's always one to think things through before acting. It's what made him a great CEO and why I'll always take his advice.

"Call into the office and tell them you will be gone for a few days and are in talks with the company. I don't like lying, but I think in this case it's warranted. Call Gary and let him know. He'll step up in your place until you get back, and I trust him."

Gary is our CFO and a good friend of the family. He's also been my biggest supporter since taking over as CEO from my dad.

"Soon as we're done with this meeting, we'll fly home and head to the office. If we need to come get you, we can, or you can still try to work your pitch. But we'll touch base in a few days," Dad says.

"Okay, thank you. Kiss Mom for me. Call me when you have news."

My next call is to Gary. I take a moment to plan what I'm going to say, but what Brice thinks is written all over his face.

"You're judging me, aren't you?"

"Not a fan of lying."

"Neither am I, but if I tell them I won't be in because I'm hurt, they'll use it against me, saying I'm not fit to be CEO. My dad never got hurt. I'm fighting tooth and nail for my job in a male-dominated world, something you wouldn't understand."

When I pick up my phone, he puts his hand on mine. "I took over the practice from my dad. It didn't matter that I had an Associate's Degree a few months after I graduated high school. Or that I was accepted into one of the top medical schools. Didn't matter that I worked my ass off to earn my degree. This town still saw me as a boy. Some here still do. They don't think my father should have handed the practice over to me. There are a few families that drive half an hour away to see a doctor because they don't trust me."

"It's not the same."

"Not quite, but I know what it's like living in your dad's shadow and having to prove yourself. I learned you can't make everyone happy. In the end, I do the best I can, and I've slowly won over most of the town. I have to be okay with that."

I nod, making this one last call to Gary.

"Hey Kayla, how was your meeting?"

"Well, I'm not quite done here. I'm in some talks so I'm going to stay a few days. Would you mind stepping in for me? There is only one meeting on the books this week."

"Absolutely. I'm so glad it's going well down there. Is the town really as small as we thought?"

"Oh, yeah, but WJ's is perfect. Send some positive vibes my way and shoot me an email if you can't reach me. Reception is a bit spotty."

"Will do. Don't worry about things here."

"With you in charge, I know I won't."

I hang up and rest my head against the headrest for a moment before opening my emails.

"What are you doing?" he asks.

"Going through my emails," I tell him as I start opening a few that look important.

He reaches over and takes my phone from me before turning onto a dirt road.

"Hey! Give it back."

"Kayla, you have a concussion. You need to relax and not overstimulate your brain. No TV, phone, or computer screens. Working is also a no. Your job is to rest and let your head heal."

I don't tell him that I can't remember the last time I had downtime since I entered school. Maybe when I was a newborn.

"Great, so like house arrest?" I joke.

"Well, I don't have plans to tie you up, but if you don't do as you're told, I just might."

His heated gaze meets mine for just a moment.

Dammit, why is the thought of him tying me up such a turn on?

Chapter 4

Brice

My alarm goes off at two a.m. and it takes me a minute to remember why I set it.

Kayla.

Shutting off the alarm, I get out of bed. I have to check on her and I know she won't like being woken up. I head down the hall to the other side of the house. Her door is cracked open and the sight of her sprawled out on the bed greets me.

She's wearing one of my shirts, which looks damn good on her. One leg is peeking out from under the covers and it's bare. Her legs are toned from those heels she wears, and I itch to run my hand along its length.

Dammit, I need to stop standing here like a creeper and check on her. Moving to the side of the bed, I kneel down in front of her.

"Kayla," I say softly, tucking some hair behind her ear. She doesn't wake up, but she does stir.

"Wake up for me, Kayla," I say louder this time and run my hand down her arm.

She moves but doesn't wake up.

"Come on, City Girl, open those eyes," I joke.

This time she moans, and a moment later she cracks open one eye and looks at me.

"What's your name?" I ask.

"Kayla. You just said it. Are you sure you aren't the one with a concussion?"

"Where are you?" I continue running through the standard list.

She turns onto her back, sighing. "At some crazy doctor's house who insists on waking me up at," she pauses and looks at the clock on the nightstand, "two a.m."

"Do you know why I'm waking you up?"

"Because you're a sadist?"

"Kayla..."

"Because I hit my head and have a teeny tiny concussion." She sits up.

"Whoa, what are you doing?" I grab her arm to stop her.

"Now I won't be able to get back to sleep and I refuse to lie here, tossing and turning."

"Come on, I'll make you some tea. My mom swears it helps her sleep."

"You're going to drug it, aren't you?"

I chuckle. "No, I'm a doctor, and not in the habit of drugging my patients. Go sit on the couch."

While I like her spunk, she really does need her rest, and hopefully, this tea will work. For the first time, I wish I had listened to my mom and gotten a tea kettle instead of heating water in the microwave.

Hopefully, she won't be able to tell the difference. Either way, the tea should help her. I set a glass of it on the end table next to where she is sitting on the couch and sit in the chair next to her.

"You really should try to get some more sleep."

"It took me a while to get to sleep as it was." She takes a sip of the tea and doesn't spit it out, so that's a good sign.

"Why?"

"Not in my bed, and I'm at a stranger's house. But mostly, my meeting with Jason and Nick. You know they thought I was some floozy sent to flirt with them in order to get the deal. It's not the first time someone has assumed that, but still."

"Well, in your heels and skirt you can't blame a guy. Around here women only wear those heels for one reason."

"What do the women around here wear, then?"

"Boots. Of which we will be going to get you a pair. They'll support your ankle and they'll be more suitable while you're using the crutches."

"So, if I had shown up in jeans and boots, they'd have taken me more seriously?"

"Maybe. Did you bore them with graphs and numbers?"

She just glares at me, so I know she did.

"Listen, you need to get to know them. Speak their language."

"I remember my dad saying something along those lines, too. You're starting to sound like him."

I smirk at her remark, but keep going because for some reason I want to help her out. "I know you did your research, but I don't think you did the right research."

"What do you mean?"

"Well, how did Jason come to own the bar?"

"He started it, I guess."

"Nope."

"I don't suppose you're going to tell me?"

"No, I'm not. You need to get to know them. Understand their family because nothing is going to happen without their family backing it. That's just how it is. You're also going to need the town on your side because we don't take too well to having a lot of tourists around here. People come in for the day to visit WJ's, or when we put on an event, but then they leave. We'd like to keep it that way."

"How do you expect the town to grow?"

"I don't think we want it to. It's a small town and we live here because it's small. After all, we know each other. If we wanted to live in the city, we'd move to Dallas."

She drinks a bit more of her tea but stays quiet.

"How long am I going to be cooped up here? And what am I going to do while you're at work?"

"Well, my dad is taking over the clinic for me. I think he was excited to step in for a few days. If you go back to sleep and get some more rest, we can go driving and I can show you around town. But we stay in the car. There will be no getting out and being overactive."

"Anything is better than being stuck in the house all day."

"You say that now."

She finishes the tea, and I help her back to bed. She's getting pretty good on the crutches, but I still want to ensure she makes it to bed okay.

Once she's in bed, I head back to my room. She's right, it's going to be impossible to go back to sleep. Not when I know she's on the other side of the house. Images of her long, toned leg from earlier flash into my mind. Would her skin be soft? How far up would she let me touch her? What did she have on under my shirt?

Before I know it, my cock is hard and wants relief. Great. Now I really won't be able to get any sleep. With a sigh, I get up and go into my bathroom, closing the door behind me. I don't turn on the light. Instead, I brace one hand on the counter and with the other reach into my sweatpants, grabbing my cock.

As I picture her laying in bed, I start a punishing rhythm. In my fantasy, I run my hand up her leg and she lets me. Then, she turns on her back, her honey brown eyes locking with mine as she spreads her legs for me to relieve her ache. Reaching under the shirt, I find her bare and wet for me.

When I run my fingers through her soaked folds, she's so responsive, and her hips move trying to get me where she wants me. Sliding a finger into her, I find her tight, wet, and warm. I add a second finger and she moans until...

Fuck! I come all over the bathroom counter. It's the strongest orgasm I can ever remember having, and it's with a fantasy and my hand. As I clean up the counter with a towel, I try to remember the last time I got laid. I have no idea. That has to be it.

I just need to get laid.

• • • • • • • • • • •

Even after my orgasm, I don't sleep very well, so when the sun starts to rise, I give up the fight.

When I go to check on Kayla, she's still asleep. Thankfully, this time her luscious body is fully covered. I write a quick note and leave it by her phone, then go out to the other side of the property where my parents live. Mom will have gone into the clinic with Dad today, but I want to check on the new cow that was born.

Normally, being with the animals calms me, but all I feel today standing in the barn is anxiety. Anxious that I'm away from Kayla. That she might need me, and I won't be there.

This is going to be a long few days.

I head back to the house but force myself to walk slowly and not hurry. A bit of space and some fresh air should do me some good. I'd love to clear my head, but every time I try, Kayla's face fills it.

Once back at the house, I start the coffee and wonder what Kayla might like for breakfast. It's barely after seven thirty in the morning, so I don't want to wake her up. Though I'm not even sure she eats breakfast, I finally decide that she seems like a simple breakfast person.

Because I want them, I start some biscuits. I'll snack on any extras with some of my mom's apple jam she made and stored in my pantry. After I decide on omelets, I go to the bedroom to wake Kayla before starting them.

I find her looking like she just woke up. Seeing her lying in bed squinting at her phone, with her long blond hair slightly messy, she looks, well, fuckable.

Dammit, she's a patient. I've got to stop thinking of her like that.

"Good morning. Do you remember your name?" I start down the same list of questions as last night.

"Yes, Kayla. I also remember you waking me up at two a.m. I'm here at your house because I supposedly have a small concussion. Anything else?"

"Nope, just get dressed in the clothes Maggie's brought you while I make breakfast. Are omelets okay?"

Her eyes get big, and I hesitate.

"Do you not like omelets?"

"I love them. Do you, by chance, have bacon to put in them? It's my favorite food and it's been forever since I had some."

"I'm a cowboy. Of course, I have bacon. Take your time getting dressed. I'll get breakfast going. Coffee is ready, too."

Smiling, I leave her to it. Bacon omelets are her favorite. I tuck that bit of info away for later and get going on frying up some bacon. Then I make extra to have on the side and I'm just serving up her plate when she makes her way to the table.

"Whew, if nothing else, those crutches are a good ab workout." Looking around, she says, "Thank you for this."

I pull out the biscuits and set them on the table.

"This is my mom's homemade apple jam. You won't eat store bought again. "

"A cowboy doctor and he can cook? How are you still single?"

"Small town. Hard to date when you know everything about each other, grew up together, and know all their flaws. I don't get out much other than the clinic, so it's hard to meet someone," I shrug.

I'll leave out the parts about picking women up at WJ's for a good time. It's how I met my last girlfriend if you can even call her that. It was more about sex for a good four months than anything. Then she said she was going to give her husband another chance, and that was the end of that.

But that was over a year ago now. Was that really the last time I got laid?

Kayla interrupts my thoughts. "What are you thinking about so hard over there?"

"Where I plan to take you today. What did you see yesterday?"

"The diner and WJ's."

"Well, there's a lot more to Rock Springs. We have a beautiful church, some shops, even a place where the town holds carnivals. We even have a small grocery store and a Dairy Queen."

She laughs then. It's a full on carefree laugh that's contagious.

"What's so funny?"

"Of course, you have a Dairy Queen! There is no such thing as a ranch town in Texas without one. But it sounds like a short tour."

"The landscape is the best part. No tall skyscrapers, no smog or congestion. Just the natural beauty of Texas. It's what keeps us coming back here even when we try to escape it."

"Speaking from experience, I take it?"

If she only knew.

Chapter 5
Kayla

After a day with no screen time, while out driving around with Brice yesterday, I had to convince him to let me use his computer for a meeting. I felt much better and I figured thirty minutes on the computer wouldn't be a big deal. Though I promised to take it easy the rest of the day.

I get ready to go to the kitchen for breakfast, which takes twice as long as normal while trying to balance on one foot. Maggie's clothes fit perfectly, and she has a very relaxed style. She included mostly loose clothes in case of a size difference. Today's choice? The beautiful blue jewel-toned maxi dress. It's comfortable and would look great on camera.

When I go into the kitchen, I find Brice making breakfast already. I feel bad he's been the one doing all the cooking. As soon as I'm able, I plan to cook at least one meal for him.

"Good morning. How are you feeling?" he asks without even turning around.

"Much better since I didn't have some crazy person waking me up at two a.m," I joke with him.

"Good. I made just plain eggs and bacon for breakfast today. Mom is thrilled you're here because her chickens are producing more eggs than she expected."

"She could sell them. Farm fresh eggs go for a pretty penny in Dallas."

"City Girl, this ain't Dallas. Around here everyone has access to farm-fresh eggs."

"Well, I was hoping to make you a deal. I know you say no screen time, but there is a meeting I really need to call into if you'll let me borrow your computer. Thirty minutes tops, then I'll stay off the electronics for the rest of the day."

He finally looks back over his shoulder at me, a look of concern on his face. But he says nothing as he plates up the food, and then walks to the living room.

I almost ask if he heard me until he comes back and pulls a chair around to sit next to me.

He shines his little pencil light in my eyes and has me follow his finger around.

"You're looking much better. Thirty minutes, that's it. Since it's right here, I can keep an eye on you."

"Deal." I feel like a kid who just negotiated the terms she wanted with her parents.

We sit and eat in silence before curiosity gets the better of me and I have to break it. "So, what are the plans after my meeting?"

"Well, I was thinking we could sit on the back porch for a while. I need to do some catch--up reading on some patient files and there are plenty of books in my office for you to read. There are even a few romance books from when my parents stayed here when they were remodeling their kitchen."

"Or you just don't want to admit you secretly read romances?" I tease him with the ease of two people who have known each other a lot longer than just a few days.

"Growing up, it was Mom who had all these romance novels in the house. But the only thing Dad read was medical journals, so I've read my fair share, I will admit."

That gives me a good laugh.

After breakfast, I offer to help with the dishes, but he pushes me away.

"Go get ready for your meeting. I'll get my laptop set up at the table for you."

"Thank you."

I go to the guest room I've been staying in and grab what little makeup I have in my purse. I always keep an emergency stash of eyeliner, mascara, and lipstick for touch-ups, so that will have to do. Wonder what the board would think if I used one of those fancy social media filters in place of makeup?

I chuckle to myself on that one. Seeing how most of the board are my father's age, I'm sure it wouldn't be looked upon too highly. Gary might like it. He's closer to my age and had a crush on me, but thankfully after I said I was concentrating on my job, he has let it be.

Since I have no hair products, I do the best I can, pulling the front of my hair around to the side so it hides the little cut there. Then I put it into a side ponytail. Giving it a little twist before securing it, I decide it will have to do. It will keep the hair out of my eyes, and it's close enough to how I wear it at work.

Well, this is the best it's going to get.

Going to the dining room, I find Brice there with a laptop set up. He's at the table reading from a tablet, and he's even thought to set me up so my back is to a wall instead of the kitchen or something else that could cause questions.

"Thank you for this."

"You're welcome. Want something to drink before you log in?" he asks.

"No, thank you. I'm going to log in early and make everyone really uncomfortable that I beat them there." I sit down and place the crutches out of sight. No point in raising questions about things they don't need to know.

"So, you're one of those bosses," he says with a hint of a joke, but I can tell he also means it.

"Kind of. Sometimes, they still don't take me seriously. They think the job was handed to me, and they would have been a better choice. It's a family company, and it was never going to anyone else. So, I like to keep them on their toes."

"What's this meeting for?" he asks as I log into the back end of our meeting system.

"My mom and dad are in New York City, and they had a meeting with a company we are trying to acquire. I guess it went well. My dad texted last night to let me know they were going out to a play and dinner to celebrate. Now, he's going to fill us in and we decide the next steps. Also, they're going to want an update on WJ's." I say with a slight amount of defeat. I have no idea what I'll tell them.

"Tell them the truth. Would it be so bad?" Brice says, replying to the last part which I guess I said out loud.

"That I'm stuck here because I chose to wear heels? That I fell, twisted my ankle, hit my head, and still didn't get the deal? Yeah."

"I see your point. Tell them you have something in the works but don't want to jinx it and you'll tell them more soon."

"Okay, I don't look sick or injured, right? Because if I do, my dad will be pounding down your door in twelve hours flat."

Brice looks at me, giving me a thorough once over. His eyes soften before he speaks. "You look beautiful."

Damn. Why do those three words make my heart race? People tell me that all the time, but it's different hearing those words from him. It's the way he says them with his deep Texan drawl and soft, ice blue eyes which let me know he means it. Or maybe, it's that he means it and is saying it to get something from me.

"Thank you," I mumble and hit the button to log in.

My dad's face fills the screen. "Sweetheart, I knew you'd be on early."

"Hey, Dad. You look like you didn't get much sleep."

"Of course not. It's the city that never sleeps."

"The city might not, but you need to, Dad."

"I told him that, but he doesn't listen," my mom calls from the background before she appears over my father's shoulder. "But, really, how are you? Where are you staying? When will you be home?" Mom peppers me with questions in the way only a concerned mother can.

"I'm fine. I'm staying at the local doctor's house. And I'm not sure when I'll be home. A few more days, maybe."

"Tell me about this doctor. What degree does he have? He isn't some small town cowboy playing doctor, right?" Dad asks.

"Dad!" I say, meeting Brice's eyes over the computer. "He's sitting right here."

"Then I want to meet him," Dad says with authority.

"I'm sorry," I say to Brice, but he stands up and joins me on the computer screen.

"Hello sir," he says.

My dad sits back in his chair and stares at him. "You're a little young to be a doctor."

"Went to Harvard Medical School. I knew from a young age I wanted to be a doctor, so I started taking college classes in high school. My mom insisted I graduate high school with my class for a sense of normalcy, but I graduated with an Associate's Degree. Took summer classes and finished medical school several years early. I had offers for a few jobs in places like New York City, but I only ever wanted to come home and take over my father's practice here in Rock Springs. So that's what I did."

"And your diagnosis regarding my daughter?"

"A mild concussion. With a bit more rest and no more bumps to the head, she'll be good to go in a few days. Her ankle is sprained, and she's using crutches. But she won't be in those high heels for a while, and assuming she doesn't try to use them too soon, she'll be okay. The swelling is almost gone this morning, so that's a good sign."

"Well, we appreciate you letting her stay with you. Any extra costs, you let me know and I'll take care of it."

When Dad says that, I bury my face in my hands and groan. "Dad, I can pay my medical bills."

"I know, but I'm your father and you're my only child. I'll always take care of you. Now let's get into business mode before these other yahoos show up."

With that, Brice takes his seat again with a huge smile on his face and shoots me a wink.

"Has Gary had any problem taking over for you while you've been gone?" Dad asks.

"Nope. I figured he wouldn't."

"When are you going to put him out of his misery and let him take you out on a date?" Dad asks, making Brice's whole body stiffen.

"Dad, I'm not talking about this. The last person I need to be dating is my CFO, and that's if I was dating anyone at all."

Fortunately, he doesn't get a chance to reply because people start signing in. They look a bit startled to see both of us, but just like Dad taught me, I put on my business face and wait to start the meeting exactly on time.

After I begin the meeting, I turn it over to my dad who goes over his meeting yesterday and the contract that was negotiated. While he's talking, I monitor who is scribbling town notes and paying attention, as opposed to those who are just there in the belief that showing up is enough.

When my dad finishes, Gary turns the meeting over to me. "Kayla, how are things going in Small Town USA?"

"They're going. Yesterday, I took a tour of the town. WJ's, as you know, features in much of the town's history, and has its roots here, so that's a big component. I was thinking each place would be unique, featuring local history and ranches instead of the Rock Springs ones."

"That makes franchising a bit difficult,-" someone says, but I didn't see who.

"Not really. The reclaimed wood wall would be the same across all locations, but the brands would be the ones from local ranches."

They launch into talking about ways to promote the locations and such, and my head begins to pound. I close my eyes for just a moment, but Brice kicks me under the table with a look of concern on his face.

"Okay, I have an appointment to get to, so I need to run. But feel free to keep chatting about all this," I say, signing out.

• • • • •• • • •• •

Brice

I'm looking at the patient records from yesterday when my dad was in the office. Nothing big, but I like to stay up-to-date when I'm not there. As I'm listening to Kayla and her business side, I'm impressed by how good she is at what she does and at gathering attention. I'd be intimidated, for sure, if I worked for her.

Switching from being a daughter to full-on business mode at the beginning of the meeting was sexy as hell. But when I glance over, her eyes are closed. I tap her leg with my foot to get her attention. Her eyes meet mine and thankfully, without me having to interject, she wraps up the meeting.

When she closes the laptop, she rubs her temples. "Maybe that's a little too much."

"Okay, come on." I stand, and not even thinking twice, lift her up into my arms.

"The couch or your bed?" I ask

"Couch."

I go to the living room and lay her down.

"You're great at what you do. But so am I, and what I'm going to do is make sure you get better. You need to take it easy, okay? I'm propping your foot up on a pillow and then going to get some ice for your ankle.

She might push herself, but when it matters, she listens to what I have to say.

Even though she'll be here a few more days, the thought of her leaving feels like my heart is being ripped from my chest.

Chapter 6

Kayla

After my meeting, I slept on and off all day and night. Then yesterday, I took it easy. It's not hard being stuck in a house when you have Brice to look at. He's handsome, especially with his dark five o'clock shadow framing his square jaw.

Today we are getting out of the house, and he insisted on buying me a pair of boots, especially since I can stand to walk a little on my ankle again. Rock Springs might not have fancy restaurants, but they do have a store that sells boots. I guess the ranching town has its priorities.

Brice parks on Main Street, and then turns to me. "Stay there and let me help you."

When I ditched the crutches today, Brice wrapped my ankle. With the flats Maggie loaned me, I can move around pretty easily. Thankfully, I'm in another maxi dress that hides my wrapped ankle.

Brice opens the door and lifts me out of his truck, tucking my arms into his. That way, as we walk into the store, I can lean on him as needed.

The moment the door opens, the smell of leather with a hint of lemon surrounds me.

The girl behind the counter just nods at Brice before going back to flipping through the magazine she's reading. She looks like she's in high school, so this is probably an easy weekend job, being as it's Saturday.

As we get to the back of the store where the boots are located, I take a look but go right to the sale section to see what they have.

"An entire store full of boots and you hit the sale section?" Brice asks, surprised.

"I didn't grow up with money. When my mom and dad started the business, things were tight. Like, living in a one-bedroom house that sometimes didn't have hot water, kind of tight. It wasn't until I was in high school that money wasn't an issue anymore, but by them, we had learned to pinch a penny like no other. I still do. Yes, I like to spoil myself with things like Jimmy Choo's, but I sure as hell didn't pay full price for them." I wink at him, and a look crosses his face that I can't read, but it's gone before I can try to figure it out.

His eyes are smiling at me in a way that lets me know he approves of my answer.

I grab a few boots and try them on. The third pair fits really well, and they have some blue thread stitched through them that I love. They'll go great with jeans, or even dressed up.

"Hey, Brice, I'm going to look at the clothes. Maybe get some jeans and stuff so Maggie can get some of her clothes back."

When he nods, I take my boots to the counter on the other side of the store. The store is large enough that Brice can't hear me talking to the girl behind the counter, whose name is Missy.

"Can I ask you a favor?"

"Sure, ma'am. What can I help you with?" she asks with a smile.

"Brice has been really helpful to me and I want to thank him. He's eyeing a pair of boots over there. Can you get him to maybe try them on and get his size? Then add the pair to my order? I'm going to check on the clothes." I hand her a fifty-dollar bill and hold my finger to my lips.

Her eyes go wide, but a huge smile lights her face as she nods. She puts the money in her pocket and goes back to where Brice is.

Looking through the clothes, I fall in love with the first pair of jeans I try on. I get them in four different colors. As for shirts, there isn't a whole lot of choice. Button down flannel or graphic t-shirts seem to be it. I get a few of each and some socks. I look around again, wondering if this place sells fancy underwear? Spotting a display of intimate wear, I grab a few of those, too. It might not be anything I'd normally wear, but desperate times and all that.

The whole time I'm shopping, I keep an eye on Missy and Brice as she gets him to try on the boots. Even from here, I can tell he likes them. Then he glances at the price tag and frowns, setting them back on the shelf. Missy stands and organizes some of the boxes, and when Brice moves to the next aisle, she picks up the boots he tried on and brings them to the counter, flashing a smile my way.

I add the clothes to the stack, and Missy gushes, "That was so much fun! I felt like a secret agent."

I laugh as she rings up my order.

Just then, Maggie walks in with two other women who are chatting and laughing. It draws Brice's attention, and he makes his way to the front of the store.

"Oh, girls, this is Kayla," Maggie says. "This is my sister, Ella, Jason's wife."

"That's why you look familiar. Nice to meet you," I smile.

"And this is Anna Mae, my sister-in-law. We're out for a sister day, kid-free!" Maggie adds.

"I love that little boy, but all he does is eat, sleep, and poop. I needed a break," Anna Mae says.

"He's only six weeks old!" Ella giggles.

"Oh, I wanted to thank you for letting me borrow some clothes," I tell Maggie.

"No problem. Brice knows how to get them back to me, whenever. Don't worry about it. You're looking much better since I saw you last."

"She's getting there, but not one hundred percent yet," Brice says as he walks up.

"Well, this is perfect timing. Sage is throwing an impromptu BBQ in light of this nice March weather. It's tomorrow after church. Come hang out, invite your parents," Ella says.

"You just want my mom to bring her banana pudding," Brice chuckles.

"I won't even lie and say no," Ella says, making them all laugh.

"Kayla is welcome, too. There will be plenty of food. Sage has been craving BBQ, and Sarah has been crazy for all things sweet, so you know those boys are going to make it happen."

Brice must see the glazed expression on my face because I have no idea who they're talking about.

"Sage is Jason's sister, who is pregnant, and Sarah is married to Jason's brother, and she is also pregnant. They're due about two weeks apart at the end of summer," Brice says.

"Jason is the oldest, and he has a biological brother and sister. His parents then adopted two more boys and Sage when they needed out of a bad home life. It's one big extended family," Ella says.

"We'll see about making it," Brice says as I turn to pay Missy.

I lean over and sign the sales receipt as Missy finishes bagging the clothes. She put Brice's boots in their bag, and I hand them to him. He does a double take at the boots inside and then looks up at me.

"I had a little help." I glance at Missy who blushes slightly. "But I wanted to thank you for everything. I know I'm not the easiest person to deal with."

A shocked expression fills his face as he knows the boots weren't cheap. But just because I prefer to shop the sales rack doesn't mean I don't have money to spare.

He reaches out, touching my arm, looking me in the eyes. "Thank you. You didn't have to do this, but thank you."

I was expecting more of a fight, but am relieved he accepted them so graciously.

Brice takes the rest of my bags and helps me to his truck. He opens my door and wraps his hands around my waist, lifting me up into the seat.

"Let's get those boots on. The added support will make that ankle feel a lot better."

Brice opens the pack of socks and places them on my feet. We both know I can easily do this on my own, but I like that he's helping, and as his fingers dance across my skin, tingles follow in their wake. When he removes the boots from their box, he places one on my non injured foot first, then gently slips on the other. It's a bit of a tight fit with the brace, but he gets it on–and he's right, the added support already feels a bit better.

"So, I think you'll be okay to go to the BBQ tomorrow. Would you like to go with me?" he asks hesitantly as he places the bags in the back seat.

"It sounds like fun."

"Well, I have a few conditions," he says as he closes the door and then gets in on his side.

"Let's hear them."

"You will be there as my guest. No business talk. Jason and Nick will both be there. This is their family, and I don't want you making them uncomfortable. You leave business talk at the door. Even if they bring it up, you change the subject."

"No worries. I feel pretty out of place here, anyway. So I'll probably hide by the side and watch."

"You'll see that Sage and Ella won't allow that."

"What other rules?"

"You're there as my guest. There will be no dancing or flirting with any single men."

I chuckle. "You make it sound like a date."

When he doesn't deny it, I drop it. But then I have a thought. This is a small town, and he grew up here. "You ever date anyone who's going to be there?"

When he doesn't answer right away, I almost think he hasn't heard me.

"I dated Sage before she and her husband got together. It's actually what made Colt stop pussyfooting around and make his move. She's a nice girl, but neither of us felt it. Colt forgave me and even included me in his scavenger hunt for Sage when he proposed."

"Scavenger hunt?"

"He sent her all over the ranch and town, reliving their favorite memories. Each letter had a clue to the next place, and it ended with him proposing."

"That is really sweet. My dad proposed beside Bonnie's grave, you know, from Bonnie and Clyde."

"What? He proposed in a graveyard?" Brice asks, shock crossing his face, making me giggle.

"My mom is obsessed with Bonnie and Clyde. Their story, the history of it. Now that she has the money, she keeps trying to get the guy who owns their car to sell to it her, but he won't. When he had it on display, the MGM in Las Vegas acquired it, and my mom was fuming for over a month. She cursed the MGM, and she cursed the previous owner. My dad has been in talks with the MGM about buying it, but allowing them to keep it on display since it draws a crowd. They haven't given in yet. It's the one thing she is willing to spend a crazy amount of money on. So, in a way, it was the perfect proposal for my mom."

"It sounds like it."

"My dad was all cheesy saying he wanted to be the Clyde to her Bonnie or something like that. Watching them tell the story is really sweet. Every time they go, they visit Bonnie's grave. Did you know Bonnie and Clyde weren't married? Their families were so angry with them, they buried them in separate graveyards miles apart in Dallas."

"I didn't know that."

"Yeah, Bonnie's is in a large cemetery open for the public to see, and Clyde's is in the small run-down one that is private. My dad has made some donations and helped to clean up his grave and get a historical plague placed so they have special access. My mother was over the moon when he gave her the key to the graveyard for their anniversary one year."

"Morbid and romantic at the same time,-" Brice smiles as we pull into his driveway.

"In a way it is, but I grew up with it, and now I just find it sweet. Everything my dad has done for her. He even said he'd play dirty to get Mom Bonnie and Clyde's car. My mom made him promise not to, though. "

"Will your dad listen?"

"Nope."

As I wait for Brice to come to help me from the car, my mom's voice filters through my head. Find a love like Bonnie and Clyde, a love you can't live without and would do anything for.

Normally some faceless man is there when I think of my 'Clyde.' Only this time, it's Brice's face.

Chapter 7

Brice

Today is the BBQ at Sage's place. We didn't go to church today, so I asked Jason to text me when they were ready for us.

Kayla was up tossing and turning last night. Her ankle was bothering her, but after some medicine, and icing it, she finally fell asleep. I wanted to let her sleep in, which she did until after ten this morning. She woke up panicked about sleeping the day away, which was absolutely adorable. It didn't seem to help when I reminded her that she needed the rest.

Now in my truck on the way to Sage's, she's staring at the scenery as we pass.

"As much as possible, I want you to sit and put your foot up. Everyone will understand, and I'm sure the pregnant ladies will join you. I don't want you to overdo it again."

"I'll ice it at least twice. Does that make you happy?" she asks with a smirk, indicating she has no intention of doing so.

"I'll make sure Sage knows you need to be off your feet, too."

"Come on, it's not that bad!"

"Kayla, this is the second biggest ranch in the state of Texas. Let that sink in. This place is huge. There is a ton to see and do, so your cute little ass is going to park it in a chair and take it easy!"

When what I said sinks in, I take a deep breath. Shit, she is going to freak out, isn't she? But she hasn't said a word, so I risk a glance at her and she has a smile on her face.

"You think my ass is cute?" she jokes.

I just groan. If she only knew what I've been thinking about when it comes to her ass, she'd be horrified to sit in the car with me.

"Every part of you is cute and you know it," I tell her.

Kayla isn't the kind of woman who fishes for compliments. She's one of those women who knows she's pretty but has brains and doesn't rely on her looks. When she got offended about Jason and Nick thinking she was sent to seduce them, that kind of sealed the deal for me. After that, I wanted to be around her even more.

"Well, it's different when you say it." Her voice is low, and she's looking out the window while talking to me.

It's probably best that she can't see what her words do to me. That she can't see how her simple confession made me hard. I shift in my seat and try to think about stitching up one of the rancher's legs that were sliced open last month. Thinking about it seems to do the trick, making my cock go down, though my head doesn't forget that we are in very dangerous territory here.

While she is here now, and as much as I want her to stay, I need to be careful because she will leave. Her life, her company, and even her family are in Dallas. She's a city girl, through and through, and Rock Springs will be too small for her. So, I can't let myself go there. I just can't.

I turn on to a second dirt road that leads to the ranch gate.

"Lots of dirt roads around here," she says.

"Yeah, Sage's ranch is the only one here, so the state has no incentive to pave it. The family pretty much maintains it. When we had the blizzard Christmas before last, they had to plow their way back into town."

"I remember the blizzard," Kayla says. "The whole city shut down. People were afraid to drive. I was in the office for four days straight before I could drive home."

"Didn't you watch the weather before going in?"

"Yes, but I was supposed to be home before it started. Then I got tied up with a meeting in China and by the time I was ready to go there was already over an inch on the ground, and I didn't have snow tires. My dad told me to stay. Thankfully, the couch in my office isn't bad to sleep on. Also, I have a mini fridge with food for my lunches, and I was able to work undisturbed because we never lost power."

"Did you at least take some time off after that?"

"Yes, I went home. Took an hour long bath and slept all day, took a second day to relax and read, and then was back at it again by day three."

I just shake my head. The woman is driven, I'll give her that.

Pulling into the ranch, I go towards the left to Sage's place where the BBQ will be.

Kayla asks, "Why is the driveway split?"

"This used to be two separate ranches. Their parents live to the right, and the one on the left they bought about ten years ago. It's Sage's family's land. A long story, but they combined the ranch and the kids all moved in over here. As they got married, they fixed up the cabins on both sides of the property. It's a big family."

I pull up as close as I can to where everyone is, and Maggie comes rushing over to Kayla's door.

"I've got her. You go park your truck!" Maggie says, taking Kayla's hand.

Kayla looks back at me, almost like asking if it's okay. I give her a nod and that seems to be all she needs as she follows Maggie into the crowd.

When I join them, I notice Nick and Jason standing off to the side as they watch Kayla, so I make my way there first.

"Mom said they would be here soon as Dad finished up at the clinic. I guess he's enjoying being back there more than I thought he would," I tell them.

"What's she doing here?" Nick cuts right to the point.

"She's here with me and promised no business talk. It seems that she and Maggie hit it off, and when we ran into them yesterday, Ella invited us. I thought it would be a good idea for her to see this, and experience the kind of community she doesn't have in Dallas. Make her understand we do things differently out here."

"No business talk?" Jason asks.

"None."

"Okay, I'm going to hold you to it. How's she doing?"

"Much better. Though she needs to be sitting down and icing her ankle. If she overdoes it, she'll get a headache. But I think being outside will help her today. Plus, she's pretty bored at my place."

"I'm sure you can find a way to keep her busy," Nick winks at me.

"She's a patient, Nick."

"Come on, you're telling me you don't have some doctor-patient fantasies you wouldn't mind acting out?"

"Go find your wife and get laid, man." I slap his shoulder and head toward Kayla and Sage.

"Sage, she needs to sit and put her ankle up," I say, walking up.

Kayla glares at me and Sage looks over at her husband.

"Colt, will you grab those folding chairs from storage? Kayla can sit in one and put her legs on another. Besides, I know I'd love to get off my feet, and I'm sure Sarah would, too," Sage says, rubbing her tiny little baby bump.

Colt rubs her baby bump, then leans in and kisses her. "Of course, love. I'll go get the chairs." He takes Blaze with him and a few minutes later, the ladies have a little circle of chairs set up. Anna Mae joins them to nurse her son, and Ella is sitting, too, with her son JJ asleep in her arms.

"Beautiful sight, isn't it?" Jason asks, walking up to me and nodding toward the girls. "They're smiling and happy. Kayla almost looks like she fits in."

He watches me from the side of his eye. Obviously, he's wanting some kind of reaction.

"I'm sure the view is nice because that's your wife, holding your son. She's here and she's yours. Not all of us are that lucky."

With a last look at Kayla, I head toward the bar to get away from the crowd. Ford catches me as he and his fiancé, Savannah, walk up.

"Hey, rumor has it you have a girl here," Ford says.

"Kayla is here. If you want to go say hello, she's sitting in the chair with the girls," I say to Savannah.

She takes the bait and gives Ford a quick kiss before going over to them. For a brief moment, I think about how funny it is that they're all interconnected. Savannah is Lilly's sister. Lilly is Riley's best friend. Riley is married to Blaze, Jason's brother. When someone marries into the family, they accept the whole family like they did when Ella married Jason. Her sister Maggie, and her brother Royce, along with her parents, all become family.

It's part of the reason even a small get together for them is still close to fifty people. To know that many people have your back is something. I've seen them stick together, and I can tell you, there are many people in town who wish they had what this family has.

"Join me in the barn?" I ask Ford, and he nods, following me.

This isn't a small barn. It's easily the size of a football field, but it's still a barn and somehow both calming and comfortable.

"What's on your mind?"

I know there's no point in trying to hide it. Ford and I have been friends since we were little kids and we've always been honest and open with each other. I know I can trust him.

"I really like Kayla."

Ford doesn't say anything right away, he simply watches me. "Like want to have some fun while she's here? Or like want to find a way to make it work when she goes back to Dallas?"

"Fuck if I know. Maybe it's just her being in my house and right there twenty-four-seven the last few days. Or the fact that I haven't been laid in a year?"

Ford lets out a low whistle and a chuckle. "You don't have to know someone long to just know. Look at me and Savannah," he says.

Savannah is a singer and was based in Nashville. She was on tour when a scandal hit and the band she was opening for suggested she take a break and visit family. That was just after Thanksgiving. So, she came here to hang out with her sister, Lilly. Then she met Ford, and they were engaged by Christmas. It was a bumpy road and not all easy, but it worked out for them and seems to be worth it.

"Again, not everyone is that lucky," I reply.

"You're overthinking it, man. While she's here, just enjoy the time with her. When it's time for her to go home, you'll know what your feelings are and what to do. Dallas isn't that far. Don't say no based on that."

"It's not just that. I looked up her company and her net worth is in the billions. She's the CEO of a very powerful company. There's no way she would ever be happy here and there's no way in hell I'm moving to Dallas."

Ford grabs my shoulders and turns me around. From here we have a view of the women and Kayla is there laughing and talking, fitting right in. With the boots, jeans, and shirt she bought yesterday, she looks relaxed and like she belongs here.

"She looks like she fits in just fine to me," he says as he watches Savannah. "By the way, nice boots."

"Thanks, Kayla bought them for me."

"I heard Missy is telling everyone about her undercover mission to help Kayla out. That woman bought you a great gift. Don't rule her out just yet," he says.

With that, Ford turns and walks through the crowd.

I stand and watch a bit longer. For just a moment, I can pretend. Pretend she belongs to me and that this is a possibility.

Too bad it's just pretend.

Chapter 8

Kayla

I had such a great time at the BBQ. The women welcomed me with open arms and treated me like I was one of them. It was a nice shift from the events I was used to attending. Usually, the people I meet are only there to network and make connections to get ahead. You don't make friends, you make contacts who will benefit you in the future.

As CEO, they always wanted to link up with me, even if they thought I was too young or didn't like me because they didn't think I deserved it or that it was handed to me. All things I've been told to my face. But they still wanted me for what I could do for them. Generally, people like them, well, really there's not much they can do for me, so I don't waste my time.

But I felt a real connection with these women. Something I realized last night I was sorely lacking in my life. I didn't feel like they would be trashing me behind my back the second I left the room. Hell, Savannah invited me to her wedding next weekend. Brice insisted I go with him. I guess he's the best man and wants a buffer from all of Savannah's Nashville friends that will be there. Can't say I blame the guy. Though I can happily imagine Brice in a tux.

That leads me to today. I need a dress to wear to said wedding and, of course, Brice knows the perfect shop downtown. It's owned by one of the ladies his mom goes to church with.

"Come on already," Brice calls with a hint of irritation in his voice.

I'm taking longer to do my hair because I want to make sure the dress goes with how I plan to wear it. But he's a guy, so he doesn't understand.

"Okay, I'm ready."

His eyes run over me slowly like it's his hands touching me all over. I wish it was his hands on me. Lord, what is wrong with me? He's taking pity on me and invited me to his friend's wedding and I'm here wishing it was a date. I need to knock these thoughts off.

"Your hair looks nice. I still don't get why you need to make sure it will look good with the dress."

"Because I don't have my hair styling stuff here, so there are very limited things I can do. Some dresses require an updo to really make them work, so If I have my hair done like this, I can make sure it all works together."

"They're just having a simple country wedding at a small country church. The bride herself will be in cowboy boots."

Exasperated, I say, "Come on. Let's just go get a dress and then I'll come home and take my daily nap so your growly doctor side can rest happy."

Brice has been insistent on me taking a nap each day to make sure I don't overdo it. Part of me wonders if he just wants a few hours a day without me around. I guess I can't blame him, as I've been in his space for several days now. I was really trying to get home to Dallas in the next few days, but now with the wedding, I'm not in a hurry.

Normally, being away from the office this long would have me in a state of panic, but with my dad back there, I know it's handled. I have no desire to rush back, at least not right now. With the excuse of the wedding to keep me here until this weekend, I plan to stay.

We park in front of a row of shops on the main street, and as always Brice comes around to my side of the truck and helps me out, even though we both know I can do it on my own. I wonder if he keeps doing it just to be able to have that brief moment of his hands on me. Because that is why I'm letting him. Horrible, I know.

When we walk into the shop, I expect to see someone around my parent's age, but the woman behind the counter is our age. She's talking to a man in a suit, so she nods to us and we begin looking at the dresses.

"Is that her?" I ask.

"Yeah."

"I was expecting someone older," I chuckle.

"Nope, and yes, my mom did try to set me up with her. We both politely declined."

As we're looking at the dresses, snippets of conversation start floating over that sound like contract talks.

"Who is that man?" I ask.

"I don't know. I've never seen him before."

While I pull a few dresses to try on, I strain to listen. Then I move to the accessories which are near the counter and closer to them.

"It's everything we talked about on the phone. You just sign it and I have a check for you right here," he says.

Something about the way he is pushing her to sign the contract isn't sitting well with me.

"Well, I don't know. This is a lot to process," she says.

"It's great exposure to have your stuff sold in Dallas, too. The city folk there will eat up your handmade stuff."

She's hesitant, and that means her gut is telling her no.

"Hey, Brice, hold these for me." I hand him the dresses I pulled.

"What are you doing?" he asks. He looks worried, and he should be.

I may not look the part right now, but I've kicked into CEO mode. Confidently, I stride over to where the gentleman is standing.

"Hey, sorry to interrupt. I'm Kayla, Brice's friend. Mind if I look at the contract? I deal with them all day at work," I ask the woman behind the counter while ignoring the guy next to me.

The relief is evident on her face. "That would be great," she says with a smile.

"Now, little lady, this is between me and Ms. Graham here and the contract is confidential," he says in his slick car salesman's voice.

I want to give him a black eye for calling me "little lady," but I know this won't help the situation.

"Has she signed an NDA?" I ask.

He laughs, but there is something else going on behind his eyes. Something I don't like, even if I can't put my finger on it.

"No, she hasn't. This is a business arrangement."

"Then, she is free to show the contract to anyone she likes. Even if she had signed an NDA, she could still show the contract to her legal representation. To not allow her to do so is illegal. Consider me her representation." I snatch the contract from his hand.

He wasn't expecting the move, so I grab it easily. When he tries to grab it back, Brice is right there. A solid wall of muscle to keep him away while I read over it. The first few pages are all standard, lining up the terms and payments, who is selling what, where the products would be sold. But buried several pages in is what he has been trying to hide.

"There is a reason he doesn't want you to read this contract. See this section here?" I point to the bottom paragraph. "It means he would have exclusive rights to sell what you make, and you wouldn't even be able to sell them yourself. The next paragraph states you are required to supply him with a minimum of a hundred pieces a month, and during the fourth quarter, two hundred a month."

"I can't even make that for myself now!" she gasps.

"If you don't, he can withhold your earnings and you would owe him for the loss of sales. I strongly suggest you don't sign this contract nor do business with this man or anyone associated with him again," I say and make a note of the company name on the contact.

"Don't listen to her! What does some country girl know about contracts?" The man tries to discredit me.

I have to physically push Brice aside because he's hell-bent on standing between me and this snake.

"I'm sorry I didn't catch your name," I say.

He straightens his back and pulls a card from his coat pocket.

"Mortimer Jenkins the Third" it reads. While the name sounds familiar, that doesn't surprise me.

"Well, let me introduce myself, Mortimer." I hold out my hand to him. "I'm Kayla Bartrum, CEO, and owner of Bartrum Enterprises. As a man from Dallas, I'm sure you have heard of us." I smile sweetly. At least I hope it comes off that way.

His face pales and he gathers up his things, realizing I do know exactly what I was talking about.

"As Ms. Bartrum said, we won't be doing any business with you. Don't step foot in my store again, Mr. Jenkins," Ms. Graham says.

Mr. Jenkins can't get out of the store fast enough and doesn't say another word. I pocket his card just before I'm swallowed in a huge hug. I missed Ms. Graham coming from behind the counter, and now she's embracing me.

"Thank you so much! You saved my business. I don't know how I can repay you!"

Brice says, "Shelia, let the woman breathe," and she steps back.

"No need to repay me, just promise to never sign a contract without a lawyer looking at it. Those snakes are a dime a dozen in Dallas.

Always trying to prey on people they think are easy targets. Particularly single females. It's better to walk away than getting sucked into a deal like that," I say.

"Oh, I swear it! I'll always have a lawyer look over any contracts. Now, what were you two doing here today? And thank the Lord you were!"

"Oh, I was here to get a dress for Ford and Savannah's wedding. Can I try these on?"

I reach for the dresses I had Brice hold.

"Of course, of course! Right this way. Whatever dress you want is on the house!"

"Oh, that is so sweet, but really it was nothing," I start to protest, but Brice cuts me off.

"That is generous of you, Sheila. Thank you."

Sheila walks back up to the front of the store and I glare at Brice.

"Don't fuss. She has a tip jar by the register. You can put the money in there, so she won't see it until after we've gone."

That I can live with. I try on the first dress and step out to show Brice. It's pink and casual.

"No, it doesn't go with your boots," he says.

This is the answer for the next three dresses until I try on the blue lace one, which happens to be the one I really like.

"That's the dress!"

"I agree."

I like that he has really put some thought into it and doesn't just pick a dress to get out of here fast. Most guys would have picked the first one.

I get a necklace to go with it and when Shelia refuses to let me pay, I slip a hundred dollar bill into the tip jar when she is distracted bagging up my stuff.

"Do you need anything else?" Brice asks once in the car.

"Nope. I'm good."

On the way home, I call my dad and tell him what happened, giving him the man's information. He promises to look into it because he hates guys like that as much as I do. I know he will do everything he can to shut him down. He's done it before.

Once we pull into Brice's driveway, he puts the truck in park and unbuckles his seatbelt but makes no move to get out.

"That was really great what you did for Shelia. Thank you. I really mean that." he says and his tone is soft, like he didn't think I'd do something like that for a complete stranger and is shocked I did.

"Of course. Though I didn't just do it because she's a friend of yours, I'd do it for anyone. I can't stand guys like that. They make it harder for the rest of us doing legit business deals to be taken seriously."

When I look back over at Brice, I swear he is closer to me than he was just a moment ago. There's a fire in his eyes and the way he's looking at me is the way I caught Colt looking at Sage a few times yesterday. Shifting in his seat, he leans over the center console and tucks a stray piece of hair behind my ear but doesn't remove his hand.

When I don't stop him, he leans in, ever so slowly giving me plenty of time to move away if I want, but I don't.

His lips barely brush mine when my phone rings. He pulls away, cussing.

Of course, my mom has impeccable timing and wonders why I'm still single.

Chapter 9

Brice

I can't remember the last time I was this nervous. After we were interrupted by Kayla's mom calling, she went and took a nap. When I tried to get some work done, I couldn't concentrate, so I tried to watch some TV. No matter what I did, my thoughts kept going back to those moments before her phone rang. She was going to let me kiss her. My lips brushed hers, and I have never wanted anything so much in my life.

Finally, after some serious consideration, I decided to take Ford's advice. She's here, so I need to make the most of it. With a little help from my mom while Kayla naps, I get everything set up for dinner tonight. I'm praying she will like it and that she isn't regretting our almost kiss. In the meantime, I'm sitting on the couch waiting impatiently for her. Though I know she set an alarm for six so she wouldn't miss dinner. But since we were out late, she took a later nap.

Actually, she really doesn't need the naps anymore. But I know she doesn't get a break when she's working, so even after just an hour, she looks relaxed and like she feels worlds better. Even though I'd rather spend the time with her myself, I keep encouraging her to take them.

After I check in with my dad to see how he's doing with the clinic, he texts back to take my time with Kayla because he's having a blast catching up with everyone. In other words, he is participating in the Rock Springs gossip tree.

When I start going through my email, she steps into the hallway and offers me a shy smile. Her hair is done up perfectly falling in light waves. While she doesn't have any makeup on, I think she looks even more beautiful than that first day with her full makeup all done.

"How would you like to get out of the house for dinner?" I ask her.

Her eyes light up and she nods.

"Put your boots on and grab a jacket. It still gets cold after the sun goes down," I tell her, and then lead her out to my truck.

Instead of heading to the road, I drive behind the house.

"Where are we going?" she asks as we bounce along the uneven trail that has been made from the frequency of my truck passing through.

"For a real country date, something that will be relaxing yet still the best food you ever had."

Even though she looks at me doubtfully, I'll prove it to her soon enough. I drive us to the spot on my parent's ranch that is my favorite. It's where I go to just think. It's far enough away from my house and theirs that you can't see any lights. At night when the skies are clear, the view of the Texas night sky is breathtaking and something many don't get to see.

With the sun getting ready to set, I know the sky is about to light up with brilliant colors in true Texas fashion. I can't wait for her to see it.

Once at the field, I park and turn on the radio nice and low. "Stay here. Let me get set up."

She nods with a small smile on her face.

Jumping out, I reach into the back seat, opening the back window so we can hear the music. Next, I grab the blankets and pillow I have stored back there and toss them in the bed of the truck.

Getting into the back, I arrange the blankets to make things as comfortable as possible. The pillows are set up for her to lean on and I place another blanket for us to use as it cools off. Jumping down, I help her out of the truck. While I know she can get in and out herself, I like being the one to do it, and it's more than just being able to have my hands on her. It's about taking care of her. Something I'm finding I want to do more and more. So as long as she lets me help her out of the truck, I plan to do it.

Closing the door behind her, I get the cooler out my mom packed. Well, both coolers. One has hot food and the other cold food. "We are going to watch the sunset while we eat. Then dessert by the stars, which should be out. Then we'll see what constellations we can find. I even downloaded an app on my phone for it," I tell her hoping she can't sense the nerves in my voice.

She lets me lift her onto the tailgate and scoots back in the tail bed, getting comfortable against the pillows. I serve dinner which is my mom's fried chicken, biscuits, and corn on the cob.

"Is it homemade?" she asks, her face full of longing as she stares at the food.

"Yep, my momma's recipe."

"My mom never cooked fried chicken. I had clients make it once at a meeting at their house and it blew me away. I've been addicted ever since."

After I make her a plate, she sets it on her lap, wasting no time taking a bite of the fried chicken.

"Well?"

"This is so good." With her mouth full of food, her voice is muffled, but she keeps eating like I'm going to take it away from her. When she swallows, I hand her a bottle of water.

"This is better than any restaurant meal I have had in a long time."

"You can't beat good 'ole southern cooking. They just can't replicate it in any commercial kitchen."

"But they sure do try."

As we eat, we talk about little things. Our favorite food, pets we had growing up, favorite music, and movies. We watch the sunset light up the sky in brilliant pinks, oranges, and yellows. When the light fades, I light a few candles on the side of the truck bed and open the second cooler. This one is filled with desserts.

"So, you had some of my mom's banana pudding at the BBQ. Now it's time to try her Coca-Cola Double Chocolate Fudge Cake. She used to try to teach me how to make it, but mine never came out like hers and she gave up. Said she'd just wait and share the recipe with my wife to make for me," I chuckle.

Kayla laughs as I serve us each a slice. I'm getting ready to dig into my piece and I'm completely unprepared for the moan that comes from her as she takes the first bite. Her eyes are closed, and a look of pure bliss is written all over her face.

When she swallows that bite, her eyes open and she looks at me. There is a small piece of cake on the corner of her mouth. Without thinking, I cup her cheek and brush it away with my thumb. Her lips are soft and tempting, but the way she's looking at me, well, it's like she's begging me to kiss her.

Before I know it, I'm leaning in and my lips are finally on hers. Her lips are kissable and taste like chocolate cake and forever. That should scare me, but right now it only calms me. When she opens up to me, I take it and deepen the kiss, my tongue playing with hers. The cake is long forgotten as she wraps her arms around my neck and runs her hand through my hair. With a jolt, I swear I feel that touch all the way to my dick.

When she lets out another one of those sexy moans, I have to pull back or I'll be pushing forward for something neither of us is ready for, at least not tonight.

We both look at each other and don't say a word. I give her a gentle, chaste kiss before settling back on my side of the truck. In that instant, I miss the heat of her body next to me.

"Eat your cake. I'd hate to have to tell my momma you never got more than a bite." I smirk, making her chuckle.

We eat in silence, both enjoying the cake. When we're finished, I clean up and set the coolers on the ground out of our way. Then I lie down and pull the blanket over me and hold it up for her.

"Come, lie down with me. I promise nothing more than kissing," I say, reassuring her that I have no intention of pushing my luck tonight. When she lies down beside me, it surprises me. Instead of using her pillow, she cuddles up against me and rests her head on my shoulder. I pull the thick, gray fleece blanket over us, making sure she's covered, so she stays warm. Then I wrap my arm around her and enjoy the feeling of her in my arms.

"I always loved looking at the stars. It's harder to see them in Dallas, but it never stopped me from trying. In high school, when the noise of everything got too much, I'd go to the roof of our building and lay there trying to see the stars. Of course, we were in the heart of Dallas by then and the lights washed out most of them, but you could see the brightest ones on a good night."

"I love coming out here. There is no cell phone service, no one to bother me, so I can clear my mind. Whatever is going on in my head, it helps me work it out."

"One night," Kayla says dreamily, "after I caught my high school boyfriend cheating on me with the head cheerleader, I was in my room crying my eyes out. My parents loaded me in the car and drove for miles outside the city limits and parked on some dirt road. The three of us lay on the hood of the car and looked at the stars for hours until I was ready to tell them what happened. I still think of that night, not of the guy but that night where my parents showed me they paid attention to me even with how busy they were."

"I could tell just from the one video call how much they care about you and how close you three are."

"We are, and it's why I made a vow I wouldn't start a family or even get married until I was able to put the time in. I don't ever want my husband or kids to feel like I don't have time for them, and right now this is the first time off I've had in five years. I busted my ass working in each department of the company. When I was fifteen, I started in customer service and worked in each department."

After I graduated high school, my parents took me to Greece. Then, for their thirtieth wedding anniversary, the summer going into my senior year of college, we all went to Paris. I started full time at the company the day after I graduated, and I haven't taken a day off since. Even on days I don't get into the office, I still work at home."

"You need a break every now and then. All that stress isn't good for you. You'll see when you get back to work you will be more productive."

The words taste like acid in my mouth. The last thing I want is for her to go back to work. Her going back to work means going back to Dallas and leaving me. But this is our first date and how crazy would I sound if I started begging her to stay right now?

No, I need her to want to stay for her own reasons. It can't be just to be with me.

Even though I have a long way to go to make her fall in love with Rock Springs, I'm sure as hell going to try.

Chapter 10

Kayla

I'm being spoiled staying here with Brice. He let me sleep and I can't remember the last time I got to do that. I'm starting to get used to it, and that can be a dangerous thing, especially on days like today when my phone keeps going off and I keep sending it to voicemail because I want to go back to sleep. Finally, after my assistant, Jen, calls me for the eleventh time, I pick up.

"The company better be bankrupt or the building on fire," I grumble.

"Were you sleeping?" she asks, making the word 'sleeping' sound like a dirty word. I guess in my world it is.

"They do things differently here, Jen. What's wrong?" I ask, sitting up and leaning against the headboard.

"The investors from China showed up today, no announcement. They are demanding to talk to you, and we can't even get to their file because it's locked in your desk. Your father is trying to talk to them, but he said you have to come in today, just for the day. In the meantime, he'll keep them busy, but you have to get here now." She says it all in one long run-on sentence making it sound like it was one long word.

"Okay, I'll have to stop by my place and get dressed as I don't have anything to wear with me."

"Hurry!"

I get up and start moving around. First thing is I need to find Brice because I still don't feel comfortable driving. It's sunny out, and that gives me a headache. Plus, after that kiss last night, well, my head is fuzzy for a few reasons.

"Stall them with lunch. Tell them we weren't expecting them, but we are happy to accommodate when I finish the meeting I'm in. Lunch is on us, and my father will know how to handle it. Have Gary go with them as he knows their file as well as I do and can answer any questions. And remind me when I get back from Rock Springs to make a copy of that damn key and give it to my father."

We hang up and Brice is just looking at me, leaning against the kitchen counter with a cup of coffee in his hand.

"How do you feel about spending the day in Dallas?" I ask.

"Why?"

I don't get a chance to tell him because the room starts spinning. I try to move toward a chair, Brice is right there helping me sit down.

"I don't think we're going anywhere today. What happened just now?"

"The room was spinning."

"Vertigo. Side effect of the concussion," he explains.

"I have to go to Dallas. The investors we have been talking to for months showed up with no notice and are demanding to talk to me. My dad could handle it except the file is locked in my desk and I'm the only one with the key."

"But your health is more important."

"Brice, I'll come back here and do nothing for however long it takes. We can't lose this deal. It's not just me having something to prove. If we lose this deal, we lose an entire department of our company. The company as a whole will be fine, though it will take a hit. But that department shutting down? It puts over two hundred people out of a job. If we get this money? I can create fifty more jobs."

"Fine, but I'm driving, and I'm not leaving your side. If you look for one second like you're going to crash, I won't hesitate to pull you away."

"Deal. My parents will be there too, so be warned. But Dad will be in business mode and Mom won't let on at work who you are."

"Go get ready. I need to call my dad, anyway," Brice says.

"Ok, dress nice, a button-down shirt at least, and keep the boots!" I call as I head down the hallway to get dressed.

For the first time in my life, I want to wear a dress and my boots to work, but I know that will raise more questions. Maybe I can implement a casual Friday or Texas Tuesday and wear them then.

Fifteen minutes later, we are in Brice's truck. He keeps looking over at me.

"What?" I ask.

"Not what I'd expect you to wear into the office."

I laugh. "We have to stop by my place first. Which will allow me to pack a bag."

"You know, now that your parents are home, you don't have to return to Rock Springs. I can get someone to bring your car up..." he trails off and won't even look at me when he says it.

"If me being here is too much, then I can figure something else out." I don't even know how I feel about it.

"No. Dad is happy at the clinic and I like being around you."

I cut him off. "Then I'm coming back. I like my doctor, plus I'm not giving up on WJ's quite so easy."

That earns me a chuckle, and he relaxes. Then he reaches over and takes my hand, holding it the whole way into Dallas. Once in the city, I give him directions to my place, a high-rise apartment building downtown. He parks in my parking spot and his truck looks out of place with all the high-end fancy cars. Though being a working day, the ones that are here are the weekend classics that the owners drive maybe once a month.

I head inside and stop at the lobby to get my mail.

"Ms. Bartrum!" my doorman, Frank, greets me. "We were starting to worry about you, but then your dad stopped by and said you were pulled out of town for a while."

"Yes, I'm here for just a day then I have to head back out, unfortunately," I reply with a smile.

"Here's your mail. Your dad picked up the rest of it and took it to your apartment."

"Perfect. Thank you." I take the small stack and go to the elevators.

Flipping through the mail on the ride up, I don't see anything important and nothing jumps out as needing my attention. When the doors open, we step into the little hallway. There is only my door and one other on this floor. I hardly ever see my neighbors, who are another business couple I've talked to once.

I open the door and step inside. The wall across from us is floor-to-ceiling windows that look out over Dallas.

"Wow, that is some view," Brice says, walking over to the windows.

"It's what sold me on this place. I work a lot but coming home at night and seeing the city lit up is relaxing."

I go straight to my bedroom and step into my closet, closing the door behind me. When I start to change into a pencil skirt, I realize I can't wear my heels. Do I have shoes other than my boots I can wear? After looking around, I find a cute pair of ankle boots. Great, now how can I dress for the office in these?

Finally, I grab a black pair of skinny jeans and a light pink blouse, with a jacket. Good enough. Then I grab a bag and toss in some clothes. Going to the bathroom, I quickly do my hair and makeup. As I start to toss those items in the bag, I stop. I don't need them in Rock Springs, and I really like that I don't have to, so I leave them. But I do grab my nighttime face cream and cleaning cloths.

I make sure to take the clothes I wore on the way here and pack up my laptop, just in case. Then I join Brice who is in the kitchen. Though, really, the kitchen, dining, and living room are all one big space that overlooks the large windows with a view.

"You have ready-made personalized meals in here," he says, looking into the fridge.

"Yes, I have a personal chef who comes in and makes stuff I can grab and eat otherwise I don't eat. That reminds me. Here, will you carry these?" I hand him the two bags and then go to the closet I keep boxes in and grab one. I fill it up with the ready-made meals since I won't be needing them, and we head out.

Instead of going to the garage, we go down two floors. There are more apartments on this floor, and I go to the end of the hall and knock. Brice watches but doesn't say a word.

A little old man answers with a huge smile. "Kayla, dear. Come in. Oh, you finally brought a man!"

"Walter, this is Brice. Brice, this is Walter. Now, I have a bunch of meals for you. I'm going to be out of town, but you make sure you come up for air and eat," I tell him.

"I will, I will. That blasted alarm you set on my phone reminds me every day," he grumbles and follows me to the kitchen. He looks at the selections I've brought."Oh, I like that shrimp stir-fry. That's a good one," he says.

"There is some meatloaf and pot roast in here, too."

"Do you have time to chat?" he asks.

"I wish I could, but as soon as I get back, we will have dinner together and I'll tell you everything. But I can leave you with a juicy hint. This handsome man here is a doctor." I wink at him, and he chuckles.

"I will wait. As long as you promise all the details and maybe some pizza."

"Deal."

I give him a gentle hug and we say our goodbyes. Once we are in the elevator, Brice asks me the questions I've been expecting.

"Who is that?"

"He is this advertising genius. In his day, he was one of the most sought after advertising experts. Many of his techniques are still used today. He's retired now and is writing his own biography. But he gets so into it he forgets to eat, so I set up alarms on his phone for that and his medication."

"How did you two meet?" Brice asks as the elevator opens and we step into the parking garage.

"There is this small little Italian place around the corner. It makes the best pizza. I was there one night, and the place was packed. I guess it was prom or one of those dances. In walks Walter and there are no empty tables, and he grumbles about the kids all taking them up. So, I offer to let him sit with me. I had a four top all to myself. Once he sat down, we ended up talking for four hours. They had to kick us out to close up. Then we find out we live in the same building."

"So, you started checking in on him." Brice helps me into the truck and shuts the door. When he gets in, I continue.

"Nope, two days later he comes pounding on my door. Apparently, he went home and looked up my company and he told me we were advertising one of our assets all wrong. He had spent two days fixing it. Hands it to me in a note and I stood there in shock. After I took the notes and read them, I decided to take a chance on it even though I still had no idea who he was.

We put the new campaign up and it doubled our income in a week. So that weekend I bought a pizza and took it down to him and finally learned who he was, and now we have dinner together a few times a month."

"Does he still help with your advertising?"

I give Brice directions to the office, "No, but he did give some of my staff a few lessons. Now he watches my company and tells me when I'm doing something wrong, but he mostly writes. I visit him because he has some amazing stories, and seems to enjoy following my life. He's like a surrogate grandpa to me."

I shrug as we pull into my parking spot upfront. "Oh, wait. They are quick to tow if someone other than me parks here."

I take a pen and paper from my purse and write a quick note and sign it and leave it on the dashboard, so Brice's truck won't get towed.

The moment I step into the building, I already feel exhausted.

Once we're in my office, all eyes are on us and don't hide that they're staring, but no one asks who he is.

The meeting with the investors is a whirlwind, but, in the end, they sign the contract. When they are on their way out, I lean over to Brice, whispering. "Get me out of here! My head is pounding."

He, in turn, whispers to my dad and a few minutes later we're back in his truck.

"I was going to take you to dinner," I tell him.

"How about I call Jo at the diner and have her make us something and we'll pick it up on the way home?"

"Sounds perfect. I'm going to nap."

"Okay, City Girl. You did great today. Get some rest."

If I did great, why do I have this sinking feeling in my stomach?

Chapter 11

Kayla

I'm getting ready for Savannah and Ford's wedding in the dress Brice loved. I can't remember the last time I was this excited and relaxed to go to an event. The few weddings I attended in Dallas were huge networking events.

I like that these people want nothing from me but to talk and get to know me. When I talked to my dad yesterday and told him this, he suggested I stay longer because if I felt that way, he was sure Jason and Nick did, too. Dad gave me a speech about how many times he would stay later than planned on a trip to close a deal he knew was right. Then he finished by telling me he had things in Dallas covered.

The only person I trust with that company is my dad, so knowing he's there taking care of things means I don't have to worry. Though I think my mom had something to do with Dad urging me to stay. Ever since she saw Brice on the video chat, she's been asking about him and it's obvious she is trying to play matchmaker. Already this week alone, she's mentioned grandchildren, and it's in ways that you know it's a setup, but you can't really be mad.

"Oh, I was at the store, and they had this beautiful Easter dress on display for little girls. If I had grandchildren, I'd have bought it for her."

Every time I've talked to her this week, she has used a version of that line. I haven't told Brice. No point in scaring him off. I want to enjoy what time I have left with him.

His eyes go wide as I step into the living room. He opens and closes his mouth to speak twice, and I'd be self-conscious if it weren't for the bulge in his pants revealing exactly how much he likes what he sees."Damn, you look beautiful," he finally says.

"You look pretty good yourself there, cowboy."

He's in what's considered cowboy formal wear since he's the best man and all. That means dark wash jeans, a button-down shirt, and a sports coat. A dressy cowboy hat, and cowboy boots—not just any cowboy boots but the ones I bought him—complete his look. That he's wearing them today of all days makes me happy. My belly does a little flip-flop knowing my little mark is on him.

When we get in his truck, he starts driving away from the town instead of toward it, so I'm a bit confused.

"You said they were getting married at the church?"

He smiles, reaching over to take my hand in his.

"The ranch church. Jason's family has been on that land for generations. They built one of the first churches in the area and it still stands today. They use it for family events. Pastor Greg will do the service there."

"I didn't know Savannah was part of their family."

"Not technically, but Savannah is Lilly's sister and Lilly is Riley's best friend, which makes Savannah family. Mike was the senior ranch hand at Jason's place before he got his own ranch and he married Lilly. That made him family and he and Ford are good friends, so Ford's as good as family."

"That's not complicated at all."

"It's a lot, but when you spend some time with them, you'll see. Rock Springs is its own kind of family."

We pull into a different driveway than the one we used to go to the BBQ and there are trucks and cars parked in the grass in front of this little country church. Its white clapboard siding looks newly painted, and there are two windows on either side of the front door with a beautiful stained glass window above the door.

Brice takes my hand and we walk in together. My heart flutters that he wants everyone to know I'm there with him. He isn't hiding us and that makes me happier than it has any right to do.

Inside the church are long wooden pews and parquet floors. Up on the stage area, there's a pulpit and another, much larger, stained glass window. From inside you can tell the stained glass has been preserved with clear window glass around it.

"Sage said you can sit with them since I'll be on stage," Brice says, guiding me to a pew with the girls I met at the BBQ.

"We'll take care of her," Sage says. "You go find Ford and make sure he isn't trying to skip town with Savannah." While it's a joke, part of me thinks she really is worried he will take the bride and run if this wedding doesn't get a move on.

Brice kisses my temple before leaving and it doesn't go unnoticed by the girls. When they all stare at me, I just shrug, not ready to tell them what is going on. Mainly because that would mean I'd have to know what's going on and I have no blasted idea.

We sit, and the moment my butt hits the pew, they start whispering questions at me so fast, I have no idea who says what.

"You're dating Brice?"

"How long has that been going on?"

"Is that why you're still in town?"

"How will it work when you go back to Dallas?"

"For me to answer any of these questions, I'd have to have a clue on what's going on between us. And I'm as confused as you are. If you find anything out, let me know." That answer seems to satisfy them–for now anyway. Maybe they'll turn the questions on Brice. I smirk to myself, thinking he's brought it on himself.

The wedding is simple and beautiful, but I have my eyes on Brice the whole time. His eyes never leave mine other than to hand the rings to Ford. Now we are in what they call the event barn for the reception.

I'm standing next to Jason's parents and start thinking out loud. "People in Dallas would pay a lot of money for space like this. Rustic barn weddings are all the rage right now."

"We use it for barn events, like weddings and holidays. But we don't rent it out," Tim, Jason's father says.

"Oh, I figured. I was just thinking out loud. Though, if you need extra money, it would be a great way to increase your income. One wedding season could net you well over a hundred grand just from renting the space alone."

Tim chokes on his drink as Brice walks up.

"You okay there, old man?" he pats Tim on the back.

"I'm younger than your father, son."

"I call him an old man, too," Brice smiles.

"Your girl here was telling me how they rent spaces like this out in Dallas and how much we could make in one wedding season."

"Yeah, she has the connections if you ever need the money." Brice nods before taking my hand and leading me over to Jason and Ella, who are with Nick and Maggie. "Hey, I was thinking maybe you should tell Kayla how WJ's came to be. She doesn't know the full story."

Jason shoots a look at Nick, who just shrugs, and Jason nods to the empty chairs. When we sit down, Jason pulls his wife Ella onto his lap, kisses her bare shoulder, and then looks at me.

"The bar used to be called Waylon's, after the previous owner. Some locals still call it that. Anyway, he gave me a job cleaning the place after school before he opened for the night. During the summer, he paid me to do repairs around the place. This was before we bought the other side of the ranch, and we were all saving money waiting for it to go up for sale. But that part is Sage's story."

Ella leans over, kissing Jason on the temple, and I get the sense this story is hard for him to tell. Brice takes my hand and gives it a squeeze.

"When I was old enough to tend bar, Waylon taught me all I needed to know. Later, he had me help with the books and managing the bar. We ran it side by side for a while. Then he renamed the bar WJ's for Waylon and Jason's. I didn't know it then, but that was the day he changed his will and left the bar to me. When he passed, his kids were pissed that I got the bar, but Waylon was prepared for that. He had a video practically yelling at his kids for abandoning him, never visiting or calling, and keeping his grandkids from him."

Jason stops to take a drink, his gaze on his whiskey glass for a minute.

"I guess they had a falling out when his wife left him for another man. The kids blamed him for always being at the bar. But it was how he supported his wife's expensive shopping habits, how he put the kids through college and paid for their weddings. I'm sure there is more to the story, but it wasn't my business. Anyway, in the long run, the judge granted me the bar. A year later Nick wanted to move back home and said he hated big city kitchens. I told him to come work for me and build the kitchen how he wanted. Jo, at the diner, wanted to close for dinner, so it was a good time for us to be open."

"Nick started entering some cook-offs in the state. He won a few smaller competitions before the big one in Dallas that put him on the map," Maggie says, beaming up at her husband, full of pride for him.

"That's about the time I met my Ella here, and we made the shift to make it family friendly. Nick's championship brought people from Dallas, even a TV show, so I made him a partner in the business. It was the best decision I ever made," Jason says.

"I think the best decision you ever made was bringing Ella and her family in to see the place. That was the day I met Maggie, and she became mine, even if she didn't realize it at first. Though she did play hard to get," Nick teases as he and Maggie smile at each other, lost in the memory.

I guess it makes sense to move forward, but keep as much attachment to Waylon as he can. It's how I feel taking over from my dad. Do my own thing while keeping my dad's vision in mind.

"It's why you don't want to franchise because you feel like you're selling out," I observe thoughtfully.

Jason looks at me before just barely nodding.

It's then I realize I have to come at this from a different angle. But I don't have it figured out yet and I don't want to think about it right now.

"Thank you for telling me that story," I tell Jason.

Again, he nods but doesn't say anything.

A couple sits down next to me and before I even have a chance to see who it is, Maggie introduces us.

"This is our brother, Royce, and his wife, Anna Mae."

I barely get time to say hello before Anne Mae is leaning in, telling us some news. "Did you hear? Another horse showed up last night."

They start whispering and I turn to Brice. "What's going on?"

"There's talk of an illegal rodeo in the area. They keep dumping half-dead, drugged horses here in town. The police don't know why they-'re still alive as they normally kill them. They caught one guy, but he hasn't given up any information."

I remember rumors of an illegal gambling ring doing something like this years ago, and shoot off a text to my dad asking him to look into it. He texts right back that he's on it.

"Dance with me?" Brice whispers in my ear, and I nod. He doesn't need words to know what his proximity does to my body. I fight the involuntary shiver as he takes my hand and leads me to the dance floor.

He holds me close, closer than some of the other couples, and his eyes are on me.

"This wedding is so different from the ones I've attended in Dallas," I say, needing to fill the silence.

"How so?" he asks, his voice low, a conversation just for us.

"Well, the big society weddings are basically a networking event. Many times, people don't even know who's getting married but they bring a gift and network. I guess it's a win for them and a win for the bride and groom receiving gifts or money. Here it's all about the couple. The guests *want* to attend. It's fun. People are actually dancing. And there's a cake with real ingredients in it."

He chuckles at that. "What kind of cake do they serve in Dallas?"

"Egg-free, sugar-free, gluten-free, taste-free," I laugh. I always pass. I only tend to go to weddings of people I know, and I eat beforehand. I'm 'still single' as they like to remind me, and I get swamped with marriage proposals."

Brice's body goes stiff.

"What's wrong?" I ask, confused.

"Guys really propose to you at the weddings?"

"Yeah, the guys with big egos who think I'm a girl obsessed with being married, and they can waltz in and take over running my company. No thanks."

When I look up at him, I don't even get a read on his face before his lips are on mine, right there in the middle of the dance floor, in front of pretty much the whole town. If Sage and the girls were wondering what was going on before, they'll be hounding us now. Even though I still don't have answers to their questions.

He breaks the kiss and rests his forehead on mine. "Have dinner with me and my parents tomorrow night?"

Chapter 12

Brice

She said yes to having dinner with my parents. That's a big deal for me because if there's any chance of something more between us, it's important she gets along with them. I wonder if meeting the parents is a big thing for her in Dallas, too. I'm sure she meets so many people she can breeze through dinner without an ounce of nerves.

That's what I tell myself, until she steps into the living room and her anxiety is all over her face. She looks beautiful, like the girl next door, every man's fantasy in a casual dress and her cowboy boots.

"You look stunning and perfect." I pull her into my arms and hold her tight. She relaxes slightly, which helps me calm down. I like that she trusts me.

"But why don't you go put on a pair of jeans? I want to take you horseback riding and show you some of the land while we're on that side of the ranch."

She nods and goes to her room to change. Last night, she had all sorts of questions about my parents. I explained that my house and land is part of the ranch Dad bought, though they live on the other side of it. While we made a road for us to go to and from each other's houses, normally you'd have to go down several roads and it could take twenty minutes from my driveway to my parents with how it's set up. She found that really amusing.

When she walks back out in jeans that hug her curves perfectly, I groan.

"What? Not a good outfit?" She looks down at her clothes.

My next words slip out without thinking. "No, I love what you're wearing. Just sayin', your ass looks amazing in those jeans." To prove my point, I grab an ass cheek in each hand and pull her toward me so she can feel how hard I am. "Though, I'll miss the easy access of the dress you had on."

We haven't gone any further than kissing and cuddling, but boy, do I want to. I figure I should at least let her know my intentions.

My head is at war with my heart. My head says enjoy it while she's here, it could be the best sex of your life and it *has* been a long time. While my heart says it would be so much more than sex, and I shouldn't even think about it unless I'm going to make this work when she goes back to Dallas.

I've been ignoring them both and trying not to think about it. She's here and I want to enjoy our time. I guess we'll figure the rest out later. Now that her headaches have stopped, she's been doing some work on her laptop. The doctor in me knows there's no reason for her to be here anymore, but neither of us has brought it up.

"Let's get going or we'll be late." I let go of her and take her hand, heading out to my truck.

I navigate the dirt road to my parents slowly. I'm used to the bumps, but don't want to hurt Kayla.

The moment we open the truck doors, we can smell my mom's dinner cooking. My guess is she's been cooking all day knowing Kayla was coming over. It's what she does.

"Whatever she's cooking, it smells amazing," Kayla says as we step up on the front porch.

I grin. "Make sure you tell her that."

I don't bother knocking. Mom and Dad would just yell at me.

"We're here!" I call once we're inside.

Mom and Dad greet us in the entryway, hugging us both.

"Now, take off your boots. You know the rules." Mom wags her finger at me before going back to the kitchen.

Following Dad to the living room, I sit on the couch. Kayla tries to sit on the other side of the couch, but I pull her to me. I don't want that much space between us. My dad chuckles but says nothing.

Mom enters the room with a tray of drinks, and some cheese and crackers.

"You didn't start without me, did you?" Mom asks.

"I haven't said a word." Dad holds his hand up in the air as mom pours us all some sweet tea and passes out the glasses.

"So, Kayla, have you always lived in Dallas?"

Before we came, I'd warned Kayla that talking to Mom would be like a job interview, and not to tell her anything she doesn't want the town to know. Mom can keep secrets about family, but Kayla is the hottest gossip in town. Since Mom is having dinner with Kayla, it makes Mom gossip royalty for the foreseeable future.

"Yes. My parents met there, and my dad started the company right before I was born."

"Ever live anywhere else?"

"Yes, Boston for school, but I wasn't a fan. The change of scenery was nice, and it was good to have some distance from my parents, but it wasn't Texas."

"Oh, where did you go to school?" Mom asks.

"Harvard."

"So, you're pretty smart then."

I glare at my mom, but she ignores me. I just rub Kayla's arm, letting her know I'm here for her.

"That's what they tell me," she smiles.

"And what is it you do?"

"I'm the CEO of Bartrum Enterprises."

"Yes, I know your title but what do you do on your day to day working hours?"

"Everything," Kayla chuckles. "I sit in a lot of meetings I don't have to be at, but potential clients like me to be there. I handle any fires that reach my desk. I have great department heads, but if it reaches me, it needs my attention. When we implement new procedures, I babysit a lot. Also, I approve all marketing campaigns and final budgets. All pitches have to be approved by me, as I deal with all contracts and investors. Since I report to the Board, it's my head on the chopping block if profit goes down in a given quarter."

Mom's eyebrows rise in surprise. "Goodness! And you do all that yourself?"

"Like I said, I have really good department heads, and by the time contracts and budgets hit my desk, there isn't much to do other than reading and signing. I have a secretary who is amazing at her job, and she has an assistant who does all the grunt work, paperwork, filing, and running around. In addition, I have a personal assistant to help with things like making sure I have the right attire for events and getting my Christmas shopping done. My dad built this company, and he trusts me with it. I don't plan to let him down."

There's a gleam of pride in my dad's eyes. He knows all about building something for your child to take over. I don't think I ever saw that man cry except on the day he put my name on a shingle next to his at the clinic.

Mom and Dad chat with her for a little longer when a timer in the kitchen goes off.

"How much longer until the food is ready?" I ask when she returns from the kitchen.

"About an hour," Mom replies.

"Can I steal Kayla? I wanted to take her on a horseback ride and show her some of the property while it's still light out."

"Of course, go, go!" Mom says, shooing us out the back door.

On the way to the barn, I show Kayla the chickens and pigs." "I told you Mom was going to be intense," I say, taking her hand as we walk.

"She'd be a good person to have on my team when I'm interviewing people. She'd weed out all the weak ones. Think she's looking for a job?"

I can't help it. I burst out laughing because most people can't wait to get away from my mom. But of course, Kayla takes it in her stride. My girl is tough as nails.

My girl?

Yeah, she's quickly become my girl, even if I really don't have any claim to her. She's here, keeping up with my mom and smiling the entire time.

We get the horses saddled, and she's getting ready to mount her horse.

"Wait. Let me help. You still need to be gentle on that ankle." I tell her.

I place my hands on her hips as she puts her foot in the stirrup and give her a boost when she swings her leg over.

"When we're finished, let me help you down off Daisy here."

"Okay. What's your horse's name?"

"This here is Road Runner. I've had him since I was ten. Come on, there's a creek down here and just beyond that field there are wildflowers, some might be in bloom."

She follows me down the trail until we reach the clearing.

"Mom loves having family picnics here when the weather is nice, and especially when the flowers are in full bloom."

There are some scattered flowers here, but nothing compared to how it will be in another month.

"It's so quiet. The whole town is, really. I guess I'm used to the noise in Dallas. Cars, horns, sirens, people. You don't have that out here in the country."

"It's our greatest selling point," I smirk at her.

We turn and ride back to the barn and unsaddle, giving the horses a quick brush before heading back to the house.

"Perfect timing. I'm about to pull this meatloaf from the oven," Mom says.

"Let me help you," Kayla says as Mom puts her right to work.

I join Dad in the living room, sitting next to him. "Well?" I lean toward him and ask. I know he and Mom talked about Kayla while we were out, and I know he'll be straight with me.

"Your mom seems to like her. Not the fact that she lives in Dallas, though. She's happy to have the gossip, but is convinced she's going to break your heart."

I look down at the carpet and nod. "I'm convinced she will, too."

When I meet my dad's eyes again, there is understanding in them. He gets that I know she'll break my heart, but I can't stay away, either. When it happens, Mom and Dad will be there for me, and that's what I have to rely on.

We're interrupted by Mom calling out, "Okay, boys, enough whispering. Let's eat."

I sit down across from Kayla, and my mom sits across from Dad on the small four top table. It expands to hold twelve, and we have used it before but with it just being my parents most nights, and me a few times a week, they keep it at a four top.

Things are quiet while everyone fills their plates and takes those first few bites.

"So, turnabout is fair play in my world." Kayla winks at me and then turns to my mom, who straightens her back. "Have you always lived in Rock Springs?"

"Yes, I was two years behind Brice's father in school."

"Did you date each other in high school?"

"No, it wasn't until he came back and took over the practice that one of the church ladies set us up."

"What did you do while Brice was growing up?"

"Helped manage the clinic's books and was a stay-at-home mom, even though I was rarely home. Brice always had something going on."

Dinner continues with back and forth questions between my parents and Kayla. I learn a lot of things about her. Like that she took ballet as a kid and was a cheerleader.

Although, my question wondering if she still has the cheerleader uniform isn't well received.

All in all, dinner is a success. I catch a smile on Mom's face a few times and one on Dad's, as well.

This woman may be destined to break my heart, but she's taking everyone around me down with her.

Once in the car, I want to shake off the night, and I have an idea. "Care to get some ice cream?"

Chapter 13
Kayla

It's been a long time since I've done something as simple as getting ice cream. Sure, I have ice cream in my freezer at home, but it's different going out and sharing the experience with someone.

Once we get our ice cream cones, he opens the tailgate of his truck, and we sit there eating and talking.

"You held your own today with my mom. Not many people can do that, you know.""I deal with mean, sexist, billionaires every day who think they own the world. Your mom is a sweetheart compared to that.. She's sweet, and honestly, it's how my mom would be with you. It means she loves you."

"That's a good way to look at it."

"Now my dad, on the other hand, he can interrogate you like the best of them. You feel like you're under investigation for international crimes or something."

He doesn't get a chance to respond before his phone rings. He frowns but answers it. "Hey, there Bill, everything alright?"

His face changes instantly, and he jumps off the tailgate. "I'm on my way. Is he safe?"

Oh shit, something's wrong. After tossing the last of our cones, we climb into the truck.

"No, don't move him. Have someone meet me at the barn. I'm on my way."

He hangs up, looking over at me. "I'm sorry to ruin our ice cream date."

At the word date, butterflies fill my stomach. It did feel like a date even if I didn't want to admit it.

"What's going on?"

"A rancher got thrown from his horse and then the horse trampled him. That was his wife on the phone. We'll beat the ambulance there."

Brice picks up the phone, hits a few buttons, and puts it to his ear. "Dad, Bill was thrown from his horse. His wife called. I guess the horse trampled him, too. I'm on my way." He's quiet for a minute. "Yeah, she's with me. I got this. Why don't you meet us at the hospital?"

"Is it okay I'm with you?" I hadn't thought about it until now.

"Yes, just be careful. With situations like this, I often don't know what I'm walking into. We don't know what spooked the horse. Could be a snake, coyote, or even the occasional bear. We don't know if they rounded up the horse or if it spooked other animals. You need to be careful with your ankle, too, okay? Promise me?"

"I promise," I say as he turns into a long dirt driveway.

"Ever shoot a gun?"

"Yes. I hit the shooting range once a month. I'm a female CEO, and I'd be stupid not to protect myself."

He nods in approval. "There's a handgun in the glove box Take it out and keep it with you while we check on him. Be my eyes for anything that spooked the horse or any animal that might be drawn to him because he's bleeding."

"Such a different life, that of a small-town cowboy doctor."

"I wouldn't have it any other way."

When we get to the barn behind the main house, there's a man waiting, a ranch hand, I guess. Brice gets the directions of where to go and the ranch hand opens a gate. Driving through the field is bumpy because there's not a road or even a wheel track, yet it's quicker than being on foot.

Pulling out his phone, Brice makes a call, checking on the ambulance and giving instructions for their arrival.

As we get closer, I see a woman waving him down next to a man on the ground.

Brice angles the truck so his lights are on the man and gets out, grabbing the medical bag he always carries in the back seat.

"Remember what I said," he reminds me.

Nodding, I follow him over to the man on the ground, tucking the gun into my jeans behind my back and pulling my shirt over it.

"He was out riding. When he got a phone call, I went out after him. I saw it all happen, but I wasn't close enough to stop it," the woman says, who I assume is the injured man's wife.

Brice leans down next to the man and begins an assessment, looking into his eyes.

"He's unconscious. He could have hit his head on the way down or possibly passed out from the pain. But I don't see a huge blood loss." Brice begins feeling the man's neck, then his arms. He pulls up his shirt up to check his stomach. Then runs his hands over his legs,

"His left leg is broken, but I don't see signs of internal bleeding. Though we'll still have him checked."

While Brice is working on making sure the man is stable, red lights fill the field.

Looking up, I see what can only be described as a makeshift ambulance in the shape of a pickup truck. More lights flash next to the barn, which I assume is where the regular ambulance is waiting.

"This is a transport vehicle for events like this when the ambulance can't get to a field," Brice tells me as the paramedics walk up.

"We need to splint his leg before we move him," Brice tells them.

One of them runs back to the truck, returning with a board and a few other items.

Then they stabilize his leg and as they work, Brice goes over his assessment on the patient, what happened, and what needs to be done using fancy medical talk. A man is laying on the ground unconscious, his wife a mess watching it all, and I can't remember the last time a man turned me on so damn much.

Keeping watch, I look around the field, but nothing seems out of place. My guess is the red lights will scare anything away.

"Any idea what spooked the horse?" I ask his wife.

"I didn't see anything. A snake maybe?" she replies.

This poor woman needs a little comfort, and without thinking, I wrap my arm around her and pull her into my side. She sags against me and rests her head on my shoulder, watching them get her husband onto a stretcher. I don't offer false words of comfort because neither of us truly knows what the outcome will be. But I can stand with her, offering my support, and remind her she isn't alone.

Once the man has been secured, Brice steps back and lets the paramedics load him into the truck. One stays with him and one drives. The woman is watching them, and I turn to find Brice watching me. The look on his face tells me he's happy I'm here even if this isn't exactly where either of us wishes we were.

"Come on, we'll give you a ride to the barn. You should be able to ride in the ambulance with your husband," Brice says.

I insist she sits in the front seat, and I take the back. I can tell Brice doesn't like it, but he doesn't fight me on it. At the barn, we stick around until the ambulance leaves and Brice goes to talk to the ranch hand.

"Did you all get his horse?" Brice asks.

"Yeah. He's a little wound up, but no injuries. No sign of what spooked him," the ranch hand says.

"Keep an eye on the horse, just in case. When your boss gets home, watch him and don't let him do too much. His leg is in bad shape. If he tries to get back out there too early, you call me. I'll come get him."

They shake hands and Brice opens the truck door for me, getting me situated. I hand him the gun and he places it back in the glove box and locks it.

It's a different world out here. Yes, it's Texas, but you still wouldn't think of having a gun in your glove box in the city. Well, at least, I don't.

"Let me drive so you can make your phone calls," I tell him since he already has his phone out again. He looks at me, and then at his phone, nods and we switch places.

The truck is a little bigger than I'm used to driving, but I won't admit that to him.

While I follow the ambulance, Brice calls into the ER and has them get ready for the rancher. I thought that was the paramedic's job in the ambulance.

Then he calls his father, who is already at the hospital, and updates him on everything. His mom is already praying with the church ladies and ready to set up a meal train for his wife, who, from the sounds of it, will have to pick up more ranch chores.

Brice's next call is to Sage, though this one surprises me. Just the fact he thought about it shows what small-town life is like. He talks to Sage about having a few guys come down to help Bill until he's back on his feet. From the sounds of it, they can't hire another ranch hand even temporarily. Of course, Sage is happy to help.

When he finishes the call, he sags against the seat. I reach over to take his hand, but he puts my hand back on the wheel and rests his hand on my thigh, which is much more distracting.

It's obvious he's uncomfortable with me driving now that his calls are done, but we have to be close to the hospital as we just reached the city limits.

"Thank you for being here," he says, looking at me.

"Of course, I'm here. I'm happy to help even just a little."

"Your ankle okay? You didn't aggravate it, did you?"

"My ankle is fine. A little sore. I'll ice it when we get home but that's just from being on it so much."

He nods, then watches the ambulance in front of us.

"Bill and my dad have been friends since high school. His wife and my mom have been friends even longer. He was always over at the house growing up, and he insisted on giving me horseback riding lessons as soon as I started walking. When I came home for my twenty-first birthday, he bought me my first drink at WJ's."

"It has to be hard knowing your patients as well as you do. I'm sure in medical school they tell you to detach yourself."

"How do you know that?"

"I watch *Grey's Anatomy*. And I might have an uncle who is a doctor," I shrug.

"I hate that. Detach yourself. It's so impersonal, and that's why I came home. I like knowing my patients and knowing their history. How they got this scar or that one. But yeah, it makes days like this hard."

When the ambulance pulls in, I park, and we head into the emergency room together. He greets his dad, and his mom wraps an arm around my shoulders.

"Come dear, let's sit down and wait on them."

Brice gives me one last look and I nod, telling him to go. I watch as he disappears through the double doors with his dad.

"Brice told me Bill is a friend of you both," I say to Brice's mom.

"Oh, yes. He's a good man. How was Bethany?"

"His wife?"

"Yes. Introductions were probably the last thing on her mind."

"Honestly, a mess, as you'd expect. She saw it all happen but wasn't close enough to stop it."

"Poor girl. Well, it's in God and the doctor's hands now."

"What's their last name?" I ask.

"Mills. Why?"

"Just wondering. Like you said, no time for introductions."

Later, when she goes to find some coffee, I step up to the reception desk.

"A man was brought into the ER a little bit ago. Bill Mills," I say to the girl behind the desk.

"Are you next of kin?" she asks.

"No, I'm not asking for information. I'd like to pay his hospital bill. Is there a way to do that now or put a down payment on it?"

She starts typing on the computer and then gives me an amount for current emergency services and an estimated rate for a few nights' stay in an upgraded room. I pull out my card and tell her to charge it and put it on file for any further expenses that arise. She does so, and I'm signing some paperwork when Brice's mom walks back into the waiting room.

She looks at me, but says nothing. I tuck the papers into my purse and walk over to wait with her. She doesn't say a word.

Brice comes in to give us an update. "He's stable, got his leg set, and there are no internal injuries but lots of bruises. They will keep him until he wakes up and go from there," he says, walking with us to his room.

We enter, and Brice's mom stops in the doorway and looks at me.

Bethany walks over and hugs me. "The nurse told me. I can't believe you did this. Thank you. I don't know how we will repay you, but thank you. You don't even know us, and I didn't think people like you existed anymore," she says, crying on my shoulder. I just hold her while everyone stares at me.

When Bethany finally releases me, she walks to her husband's side.

"What was that about?" Brice asks, approaching me with his parents.

"She paid for his room," his mom says.

I look away because I was hoping to do this without the big hoopla.

"Did you?" Brice asks.

I sigh. "He's a friend of yours. I figured if he couldn't hire a ranch hand to help out, the medical bills would be a burden, so I took care of them. Now can we drop this?"

They do, and we stay for a little bit before giving Bethany her space and leaving for home.

Once we're back, Brice takes me to the living room and sits on the couch, pulling me into his lap. Wrapping his arms around me, he says, "I just need to hold you.".

Not want, but need. So, I know I'll sit there as long as he needs me. He's stressed and tense and I wish there was something I could do.

"What do you do for stress relief around here?" I ask.

He looks at me with a smile. "We go mudding, City Girl."

Chapter 14

Brice

Mudding is the perfect way to de-stress. I still can't believe Kayla has never been mudding. I thought it was a rite of passage for every Texas teenager, even those living in the city.

"What? I spent my free time working with my dad. Instead of football games, I would attend business dinners, and instead of school dances, I went to charity galas and networked."

It's not the first time I've realized how far apart our worlds are. But today is about having fun, so I push it away once again and try not to think about it.

"Well, this place is on Jason's family ranch. Many of us would come up here on weekends and hang out with them. They had a shower in their barn and we used it, and then his mom would feed us dinner on the back porch before we went home."

"That sounds perfect," she sighs, a faraway look in her eyes.

I pull up at the ranch and pass Jason's parents' place. His mom waves from the porch, so I slow and put my window down.

"How's Bill?" she asks.

"I got the call this morning that he woke up, so things are good. He'll stay a few days in the hospital before he heads home. After he heals, he'll need some physical therapy before he's back to full speed," I tell Helen.

She rests a hand on her belly and lets out a sigh of relief. "It's every ranch wife's nightmare, you know," she tells us with a frown. Waving us off, she adds, "You kids have fun."

I continue to the mudding pit that is set up near the creek. When we get there, Jason and his brother already have the four-wheelers out and music going.

When I park, Jason meets us. "Mom took the kids so we're all here. The pregnant ladies can sit on the tailgate. Have fun. The yellow one is yours," he says, nodding toward the four-wheelers.

"Ready?" I ask Kayla, turning to see her with a big smile on her face.

One thing I really like about her is that she makes it easy for me to forget everything else so I can just pay attention to her. Right now, I'm focused on the day and the fun ahead.

Hunter and Megan are already covered in mud, and Jason and Ella are getting ready to go in. Lilly and Mike are here, as are Maggie and Nick, and Blaze and Riley. It will be a fun day.

"Guys drive first, then we'll switch and let you girls have a bit of fun," I tell her, taking her hand as I lead her to the four-wheeler Jason said we could use.

I swing a leg over and start it up, but Kayla just stands there staring.

"Come on, City Girl. Don't chicken out on me now."

She hesitantly climbs on behind me and lightly places her hands on my hips.

"You need to hold on tighter than that." I pull her arms tight around me. I'm not going to lie, a big draw of mudding today was to get her arms around me and her chest pressed against my back. I really can't wait until we switch, and I can wrap my arms around her.

She holds on tight, and we take off. I start slowly, letting her get used to it, but once I feel her relax a bit, I speed up. When the other guys spray mud our way, she buries her head against my back but is soon laughing nonstop. Every time I look back at her, there's a big grin on her face. The tension from the last few days fades away by the time the girls are ready for their turn to drive.

Stepping off the four-wheeler, I get my first good look at Kayla. She's covered in mud, but she looks so damn beautiful. Her smile lights up her face as she takes her seat on the four-wheeler, and I slide in behind her. I don't leave an inch of space as I press my chest to her back and wrap my arms around her.

"Don't go easy on them City Girl, and I'll have a special reward for you when we get home," I whisper in her ear, and a shiver runs through her body.

Knowing I have that kind of effect on her is a huge turn-on, a fact I don't hide from her as I press my erection into her back. She freezes for a second, then wiggles against it. That small amount of friction feels so good that I can't hold back a groan.

"Better get a move on," I tell her before I give in to the temptation to drag her back to the truck and take her home to ravish her.

She lets out the sweetest giggle and takes off on the four-wheeler like she's been driving them her whole life. She is slow at first, and everyone seems to be giving her space to learn what she's doing, but as soon as she sprays Blaze and Riley with mud, it seems all bets are off. By the time the girls call it quits, the sun is starting to set.

"Best go get cleaned up so we can eat dinner. Brice and Kayla, you guys rinse off at the barn by my parents. We'll take care of the four-wheelers," Blaze says.

"The goal is to get most of the mud off, and we'll shower back at the house. So make it quick," I tell her.

I let her have the shower stall, but I strip to my boxers behind the barn and use the hose to rinse off. I want to get her home and to myself as quickly as possible. Thankfully, she steps out about the same time I'm done switching out the towels in the truck.

The drive home is quiet, and the entire way she holds my hand. We both know what's coming as we weren't shy about teasing each other today. When I park the truck, I finally look over at her.

"If you want to stop or take a pause, now is the time to do it."

She shakes her head, "I don't want to stop or even take a break."

"Okay. Come take a shower with me."

She nods, so I help her from the truck and pin her to the side with the kiss I wanted to give her back at the mudhole. She melts into me, and I pull away only to lead her into the house.

I don't get further than the front door before I have her pinned to it and my lips are back on hers. She pulls me closer, wrapping her arms around my neck. When she runs her fingers through my hair, it's almost too much to take. I feel it all the way to my cock, which is hard and starting to leak.

Without wasting any more time, I start moving us toward my room. Before we even make it to my bedroom door, we're out of our boots and both our shirts are gone.

Her back hits the door and she pulls me into her, her lips never leaving mine. It takes every ounce of control I have left to stop kissing her long enough to remove our pants. The moment my pants hit the floor, she pulls me back in for another kiss.

When she wraps her legs around my waist, I carry her into the bathroom. I set her on the counter, and she lets out a little squeal when the cold granite hits her skin. I break the kiss just long enough to turn the water on and let it warm up before my lips are back on hers.

Removing her bra, I take a moment to enjoy her luscious breasts with their pink nipples peeking up at me. I cup them, running my thumbs over the peaks of her nipples. When she moans, I swear my dick gets harder. How, I have no idea because I don't think I've ever been this hard in my entire life. Finally, I remove the blue lace panties that match her bra. Then I get my first look at Kayla in all her naked glory. It's a sight to behold.

Her delicate bronzed skin is soft, her muscles toned, and even standing here, I can see how wet she is.

"Last chance to back out and go shower in your own bathroom," I tell her.

She shakes her head. "I want this. I really want this," she says before reaching for my boxers and pulling them down.

My cock springs free and points right at her. He knows what he wants, too. I take her hand as she slides off the counter and lead her into my large walk-in shower. I've never been so happy I put in the dual shower heads when I renovated it as I am right now. Having the warm water rush over us while I run my hands through her hair, knowing the water is keeping her warm, was worth the additional cost.

She tilts her head back, letting the water run down her face before she opens her eyes and looks at me.

I grab my soap and slowly start washing her. Starting at her shoulders and down to her arms, then across her chest, I pay special attention to her perky breasts and belly before turning her to do her back.

Then I kneel down and cup her ass before spreading her legs and washing them slowly, getting close to her center but never touching it.

"Bend forward. Hands on the wall, legs spread," I order her.

She looks over her shoulder at me but then does as I ask.

Gently, I place my finger over her slit. "Good girl," I praise her, making her pussy throb.

Spreading her legs even wider, I lean in to get my first taste of her. When my tongue hits her clit, she sags forward, giving me even better access to her. Gripping her ass and spreading her round globes apart, I give her a few more licks, but as much as I want to stay down here, if I keep going, I'm going to cum all over the shower floor.

Instead, I turn her back against the shower wall. I should lay her down in bed and take my time but I'm not going to make it out of the shower. When she wraps her legs around my waist, her pussy is right there rubbing against my cock, and it's all I can do not to take advantage and plunge inside her slick entrance.

"Shit, I need to get a condom." I move to put her down, but her legs tighten around me.

"I'm on the pill, have been since I was sixteen. I haven't been with anyone in years. I'm clean," she says and once again I'm fighting for control over my cock.

"I haven't been with anyone in well over a year and I was tested since then. I'm clean, too. But are you sure you want this? We can move to the bed."

"I want it here, just like this," she pants, tightening her legs again pushing her warm center against my aching erection.

Keeping my eyes locked on hers, I slowly slide into her moist heat for the first time. She's everything I imagined, warm and tight, fitting me perfectly. When I'm fully seated inside her, a feeling of completeness washes over me. It hits me hard in the gut and almost causes my legs to give out.

Pinning her hard to the wall, I start a slow rhythm to drive her crazy. I want this to last as long as possible. Her nails dig into my shoulders and the next minute her hands are in my hair.

Her boobs tempt me, and I lean forward and suck a her hard nipple into my mouth. She groans, and her pussy tightens on me. I reach between us and start to play with her clit because I know I won't last much longer, and I need her to come before I do. Playing with her clit causes her back to arch, pressing her breasts against me. A few more thrusts and she is cumming, clamping down on my cock, and the strength of her orgasm triggers mine.

We sag against each other with satisfied smiles on our faces.

When I can move again, I turn off the water, saying, "Let's dry you off because I have plans to do that again."

Chapter 15

Kayla

I crack open an eye and realize I'm not in my room, or rather, the guest room. It takes a minute to remember the mudding, the shower, and ending up in his bed. I turn on my back and the arm slung over my body pulls me closer. He doesn't look awake, and I love that even in his sleep he wants me near him.

That's when I hear it again. The noise that woke me up is someone pounding on the door.

"Brice, someone is at the door."

"Tell them to go away. I have plans to be inside you all morning." He kisses my shoulder.

"Okay." I roll out of bed and pull my underwear on and his t-shirt. I try to fix my hair on the way to the door, but since I ended up in bed with it wet, I don't think there's any hope for it.

Whoever it is starts pounding on the door again. I open it expecting to find one of Brice's friends, or even a patient, but instead both my parents are standing there. They stare me down and there is no mistaking what they woke me up from.

"Brice, I don't think we're going back to sleep," I yell, stepping back to let my parents into the living room. A moment later, Brice almost stumbles in wearing sweatpants and pulling on a t-shirt, his dark brown hair a mess.

Thankfully, he recognizes my parents from the video call and stops in his tracks.

"Did we know they were coming?" he asks me.

"Nope."

He looks at me and his eyes soften. I can tell he likes me in his shirt, but he can't do anything about it. "Go get dressed. I'll make coffee and breakfast."

I nod and turn toward my room, while he goes into the kitchen and my parents take a seat on the couch.

When Brice steps into my room with a cup of coffee, I'm dressed and running a brush through my hair.

"I liked you in my shirt. You'lll have to put it back on again tonight." He kisses my neck, sending shivers through my body that make me want to ignore my parents and drag him back to bed.

"Oh, *that* shirt?" I nod to the shirt I placed on my bed.

"Yes, that shirt." He palms my ass, and I have to brace myself on the counter.

"That shirt is now mine. You won't be getting it back."

"Mmm, I like the idea of you sleeping in it." He nuzzles my ear. "But we better get back out there, or your parents will know exactly what we're doing in here."

Then he walks out as if nothing happened.

Asshole.

He knew exactly what he was doing to me. Now I'm hot, bothered, and wet, and still have to go out there and entertain my parents, possibly all day before I can drag him back to bed.

How did he not walk out of here with an erection?

After taking a moment to get myself under control and fortify myself with a few sips of coffee, I walk out to the living room.

"What are you wearing?" my mother asks.

I look down and find myself in jeans and a flannel shirt I got from the store when we bought our boots.

"Clothes. When in Rome," I shrug, and my mom shakes her head but doesn't say anything more.

Brice is smirking at me from behind his coffee cup. I sit on the other side of the room from him, which earns me an instant frown, but he doesn't comment.

"Mom, Dad. What are you doing here?" I get right to the point.

"We're here to check on you dear. It's like you dropped off the face of the planet," Mom says.

"I should be shocked you found Brice's address, but I'm not. Why didn't you just call?"

"That's my fault. I had some information about the horses you had me look into and I knew you'd want it right away," Dad says, handing me a file.

I glance at Brice before taking the file and flipping through it. Instantly, I know it's from Dad's private investigator. It's full of notes, reports, photos, background checks, and police reports. Not all these photos are recent. Some go back months, which means they were taken from another source. There are even some security cam photos.

I take the folder over to Brice. "Any of these horses look like the ones that showed up here?"

He looks at me with so many questions in his eyes but sets his coffee cup on the end table and takes the folder, flipping through it.

"That is Black Diamond. I'm sure of it. She was the first one to show up." He flips through a few more. "This is Snow White. She was pregnant when we found her. And this is Ford's Whiskey, I know that mark. Where did you get these?"

"My daughter told me about the rumors of the illegal rodeo going on here and what happened. It sounds like a ring that was busted about six years back, so I did some digging. Money buys you a lot of things, not all of it legal. While some choose to use it for things like that, I choose to use my money to catch people like this."

Brice hands me the folder and I look through it again. "You sure you want to do this, Dad? There are some really high ups in here. They could try to retaliate and hurt us."

"I thought about that already and I have a few precautions in place. But we'll be fine, other than having to explain how we got some of this information. All I have to say is I was approached, and it sounded off, so I did some digging. This is what I found and turned it over to the police. At most, I'll face some fines which I'm okay with."

I trust my dad. If he says we will be fine, then I know we will be.

"Do you know the cops on the case here in Rock Springs?" I ask Brice.

After staring at me in shock for a moment, he pulls out his phone and makes a call. Then he goes to his room to finish getting dressed.

About ten minutes later, a state trooper shows up at the door. Brice greets him and invites him in.

"This is Miles. He's been assigned here to crack this case," Brice introduces us.

Miles takes a seat in the chair I was sitting in earlier. When I sit next to Brice in the love seat, everyone looks at me, so I guess I'm taking the lead on this.

"I was told about the illegal rodeo and the horses showing up. Because I'm not from around here, this is the first I'd heard about it."

Miles pulls out a notepad and pen. "May I ask where you're from?"

"Dallas. I'm Kayla Bartrum, CEO of Bartrum Enterprises."

"And why are you in town?"

"I've been talking with Jason and Nick at WJ's about working with them, possibly franchising. During our last meeting, I took a spill in the parking lot, hurt my ankle, and hit my head. I wasn't able to drive back to Dallas, so Brice here was kind enough to take care of me and let me stay here while I recover."

Miles nods, making notes.

"Anyway. When I heard about the horses, I sent the information to my father who was back in Dallas. It sounded a bit like something that had been broken up several years back. After he looked at what I sent, he brought the file here for Brice to look at. Brice just verified some of the horses in these photos as the same ones that have randomly shown up." I hand Miles the file my dad brought.

Miles looks at it and then takes it from me. "How did you obtain this formation?" he asks before opening it.

"From a private investigator. Someone I used to break up the last ring," Dad replies.

Miles frowns. "You were involved in breaking up the last ring?"

"Yes. I'm sure you know from our name we are one of the most influential families in Dallas. We get approached all the time about investments. I always do my research after talking to someone. Both times my research has led me here," Dad replies.

Miles nods and finally opens the folder in his lap. Brice wraps an arm around my waist and pulls me to his side. A move my parents notice but don't comment on. I know they'll wait until Miles leaves before saying anything to us.

"Which horses did you recognize, Brice?" Miles asks, his eyes still on the contents of the folder.

"Black Diamond, Snow White, and Whiskey."

"Who is Whiskey?"

"The one Ford got from Mike. He was the last one to show up at the church," Brice explains.

"This is crazy," Miles says. "We thought it was some hillbilly rodeo or people gambling away their mortgage. This." he shakes his head, "this is bigger than anything I've ever seen. You'll testify how you got this information?"

"Of course," my dad says.

Miles looks at me.

"I'll testify to whatever you need," I nod.

"Okay. I'm sure my boss will want to talk to all of you."

"Well, I'll be heading back to Dallas this afternoon." Dad pulls out his business card. "Call me. I'm happy to meet up anytime."

Miles looks at me and I get tongue tied. I glance at Brice, who seems just as interested in my answer as my parents.

"I'll be in town for a little while longer,-" is all I offer, but it seems good enough for Miles because he stands, says his goodbyes, and leaves.

"So, we never did get breakfast. How do you feel about brunch?" Brice asks.

"That would be nice," Mom says.

"Why don't we go chat on the back porch?" I suggest as Brice goes off to make brunch.

As they go outside, I stop and refill my coffee.

"I'm glad you're staying," Brice says.

"You might not be after my parents are done with you. They picked up on everything today, and while they may not have said anything in front of Miles, I'm about to get an earful. Then you'll have your turn, too."

"I'm looking forward to it," he says with a chaste kiss before I join my parents on the porch.

"I see why you haven't been in a hurry to rush back home," Mom says.

"That wasn't it at first. But now, it's part of it." I don't bother lying to my parents. They can tell when I'm lying, and it just wastes time. They are always honest with me, so I always try to return the favor.

"What's the other part?" Mom asks.

"Brice has been helping me get to know Jason, his family, and the town. Yesterday we went mudding with Jason and Nick, their wives, and some of their family."

"Mudding?" my mom asks like I just told her I sold a kidney on the black market.

"It's what they do around here," I laugh. "-Once you get past the mud part, it's actually pretty fun. Jason and Nick have opened up and told me how WJ's came to be, and some of the not-so-public history. I'm understanding it better and I now know my pitch was all wrong."

"You think this deal is worth all this time and energy?" Dad asks.

"In reality, probably not. But I need this. I can't walk back in there empty-handed and I've more than earned some time off," I say, looking through the kitchen window where Brice is chopping some vegetables.

"How do you justify it to the Board, to your employees?"

"When I get back, I'll tell them I was injured. But they don't need to know that now. I'm working on a business deal and that's it. You were gone for three months in Europe my freshman year of high school, closing a business deal."

"Worst fucking three months of my life," he growls and pulls my mom to his side, kissing her. "But sometimes you have to shift gears for the better of the company you're working with."

I know how miserable they were apart.

"Listen," I say. "Business-wise, is this the best thing? I don't know. But I've watched you two my whole life, and as driven as I am, I still want what you have. I don't know if that's with Brice, but I've never felt about anyone the way I do about him, and I'm not willing to walk away just yet."

"Then I guess it's time we officially have our talk with him," Dad says.

Chapter 16
Brice

It's been a few days since Kayla's parents left and I feel like she's pulling away. Yesterday, she suggested I go into the clinic like she didn't want me around. She's been working more than before.

Miles and his team moved fast. With the help of Kayla's dad, they got someone in undercover and busted the place up yesterday. That didn't seem to change Kayla's mood like I was hoping. The only thing I keep coming back to is the brunch with her parents didn't go as well as I thought it did.

While I cooked, they talked, and then, just as Kayla predicted, her parents grilled me while we ate. I didn't mind. She survived dinner with my family, and I know her family did it because they care. I thought it went well. Her parents were smiling, and by the end of the night, we were all laughing.

The following morning, Kayla pulled out her laptop and started working. I keep telling myself if she didn't want to be here, she would just make an excuse and head back to Dallas. But she hasn't done that, so it's a good thing.

Right now, watching her on the computer, I can see she is irritated at something. She hasn't looked up from the computer or spoken to me in hours, so I figure one last ditch effort before I suggest maybe she should go back to her office to work.

"You've been attached to the computer for days. Let's go out tonight. Maybe have dinner at WJ's. They have a live band tonight."

At my words, she finally looks up at me, and the tension in her shoulders eases as she stretches her neck side to side as if realizing she hasn't moved in hours.

"Yeah, that sounds good," she agrees, finally closing the laptop.

"Go get ready. We'll leave soon."

I watch her head off to her room, where she has been sleeping for the last few nights. Her reasoning is that she's been working late and didn't want to wake me. I've told her several times, I don't care if she wakes me, I just want to wake up with her but I still wake up alone the next morning.

While waiting for her to change clothes, I check my email on my phone. Nothing important, but it's a habit.

"Is this okay?"

I look up to see Kayla in a sundress that ends at her knees, and she's wearing her cowboy boots. Her blond hair is pulled back, her brown eyes sparkle, and she looks stunning.

"It's perfect."

She offers me a smile, but it doesn't quite reach her eyes.

The drive to WJ's is quiet, and when we get there we grab a table.

"Whatever that smell is, it's amazing," she says as our server walks up.

"It's the BBQ brisket special," the server smiles.

"That's what I'll have," she replies.

"Make that two." I hand the waitress the menus.

"Well, that was easy. Drinks?" she asks.

We rattle off our drink orders and she leaves.

I decide to bite the bullet. "What did your parents say to you to have you attached to your computer the last few days?"

"Basically, I've been a bit too detached since being out here. Dad's right. I was ignoring almost everything. I'm the CEO and I can't do that."

"So, you work yourself to death and ignore me?"

Her eyes meet mine and I think she is about to yell or scream, or maybe tell me I'm overreacting.

"I tend to do that. When I get lost in work, I don't realize how much time passes. You have to call me on it. Like tonight. It's just how I am. I'm used to my assistant coming in and reminding me to eat or when I have a meeting. It breaks things up. I don't have that here."

"Why haven't you been coming to bed with me as I asked?"

"I didn't want to wake you up."

"Come on, I told you I didn't care if you woke me up. What's the real reason?"

The server comes and sets our drinks down. Kayla takes her time having a few sips like she is trying to find the right words.

"I've never shared a bed with anyone. That night after the shower was the first time I woke up next to someone. I haven't had a relationship since college and even then, I was always so busy I never spent the night."

The anger and worry melt away. She's new to all this, and that I can work with. Reaching across the table, I take her hand in mine and squeeze it. We chat a bit before our dinner arrives.

"This is so good," she moans after her first bite. A sound that goes right to my dick.

"This is the reason people drive all the way from Dallas for Nick's food," I agree.

We both finish every bite on our plates, and for a little thing like her, it's impressive. But the food is so good you don't dare let it go to waste.

"Dance with me? We can work off some of that food," I joke as she takes my hand and lets me lead her onto the dance floor.

Pulling her into my arms, I hold her close. "I hated the distance between us these last few days," I murmur into her ear.

"Me, too." She rests her head on my shoulder, a move that feels like home. This is where she's meant to be.

"I'm not going to let you get sucked into work like that again."

"I hope you don't. I don't like it and I end the day feeling horrible."

"Of course, I have special ways of distracting you." I nip at her ear causing her to giggle. After the last few days, it's a sound that soothes my soul.

As we dance, more and more people join us. It gets crowded, but neither of us has plans to end our dance as one song changes into another. The couple next to us starts talking about the brisket and the man says he wishes he could buy some BBQ sauce to take home with him.

Kayla lifts her head, looking at me, and I know her wheels are turning,

"Sometimes you have to shift gears. That's what my dad said."

"Maybe this is your sign."

"Yeah, maybe." She smiles, snuggling back into me.

Even as I'm holding her close, something in my gut is saying this is the beginning of the end.

When the song is over, I lead her to the bar to get something to drink. We sit down and Jason walks up.

"You hear they finally shut down that illegal rodeo? It's all the locals are talking about tonight," Jason says.

"Yeah, it's going to be a shit show in Dallas," Kayla says. "There were some politicians involved, some CEOs, people on the mayor's staff, and even a few members of the police force, which is how they stayed under the radar for so long. Also, there was a huge land developer involved. My dad is already trying to figure out how we can scoop up some of the companies that will go under because of this."

"Rumor has it, it was you who put the pieces together," Jason says.

"When I heard the story, I had my dad do some digging. He was able to get some people in there to help bust it up."

"Well, however it was done, we all thank you. The horses going missing outside of town was causing a lot of tension and stress. People will sleep a bit better tonight, for sure."

"Well, I'm glad I could help. In other news, I had an idea for something different. If you have time this week, I'd like to pitch it to you and Nick. But I still have to do some research."

Jason hesitates. I know he doesn't want to be rude, but at the same time, he doesn't seem open to any of her ideas after the franchise one.

"I think this is a good one, Jason."

"Okay. For you, Brice, I'll take this meeting."

"You won't regret it," Kayla says.

"Oh, I don't know about that. Something tells me I will," Jason says wryly.

We hang around for a little longer before I say, "Let's head home. It's been too long since I've had you in my bed. I just need to hold you."

I can't get us home fast enough. Kayla seems to be back to her old self, and I'm kicking myself for not talking to her sooner. Lesson learned as they say.

Once home, she gets ready for bed and joins me wearing nothing but my shirt, standing in the doorway looking shy. Climbing into bed, I hold the blanket up for her.

"Come on, climb on in," I tell her, and she does.

I pull her to me, her back to my chest, and hold her, wrapping my arms around her.

"How am I so addicted to sleeping with you after just one night?" I whisper.

"I don't know. I slept so good with you, but the last few nights were horrible," she says.

"Even though I'm pretty sure you're scared, I hope you trust me."

"I trust you."

We lay there for a few minutes, enjoying each other. After a while I smooth my hand up and down her arm, just appreciating the feel of her soft skin. But simply having her this close is turning me on. I'm sure she can feel my erection nudging her, but I don't make a move in that direction.

Instead, I reach down and slowly stroke her leg. Her skin is smooth and with each touch, I move up a little higher until I'm inching under the shirt she is wearing. She doesn't stop me, and her breathing quickens.

A few more strokes and I find she isn't wearing any underwear. My cock throbs, but I don't say a word, not wanting to break the spell. When I move up the inside of her thighs, I find her pussy drenched. This time I pull her leg up and back resting it on mine, opening her up for me. I trail my finger back up the inside of her thigh to her center and start stroking her.

"I love how wet you get for me," I whisper hoarsely in her ear.

That seems to break the spell because she wiggles her hip against my cock.

"I love how hard you get for me," she moans.

I play with her clit, slowly teasing her until she is whimpering before thrusting two fingers into her.

When I continue thrusting my fingers into her, she lets out a low moan. She's laying with her head on my other arm, but I'm able to reach around and play with her breast. The shirt might be covering it, but her nipples are so hard there is no hiding them.

As much as I'd love to have her remove the shirt so I can see them, I have plans to fuck her in it. Just thinking about her in my shirt while my cock is inside her has me rock hard.

Without losing a beat, I replace my fingers with my cock on the next thrust. She gasps and arches her back, pushing her ass into me and causing me to sink even further into her. She is so wet I slide right in.

"This isn't going to last long. I've been craving you for days, having you so close but not being able to make love to you. No more of that shit. I want you in bed with me every night. No excuses." I start stroking her clit nice and slow. "Promise me you will sleep in my bed."

She doesn't answer me, so I stop all movements.

"Promise me," I say again.

"I promise, Brice. I missed being in your arms even if I was scared to be here," she cries out.

I continue my thrusts and it isn't long until she's falling over the edge and taking me with her.

Making her come and having her promise to be in my bed every night doesn't do anything to diminish the feeling in my gut that things are about to change.

Chapter 17

Kayla

I'm awake as the first ray of sunlight filters through the room. There are so many ideas running through my head for Jason and Nick, but I need to have my data straight and everything worked out before scheduling the meeting. Slipping out of bed before Brice wakes up, I go to the kitchen to start the coffee. I toss my hair up in a messy bun, grab my computer, and sit down at the dining room table.

With my coffee in hand, I start pulling the data I need and shooting off emails to get the stuff I can't find myself. Then I send a few texts to Sage for help on a few things. Thankfully, she's up early, too, and more than happy to help me out once I explain what I'm doing.

As always when I'm working, I lose track of time until Brice enters the kitchen and walks over to me. I turn my attention to him crouched down beside my chair.

"I didn't like waking up alone."

I tug him in for a kiss, and when he tries to deepen it, I pull back. "I couldn't sleep. With all these ideas for Jason and Nick in my head, I had to get started on them. I promise I'm not going to lose myself in work today."

He looks a bit skeptical but leans in for another kiss. "Have you eaten yet?" he asks.

"No, but there's coffee."

He gives me a scolding look before heading into the kitchen to make some breakfast.

As he starts plating food, I close my computer, a move I know doesn't go unnoticed by him.

"Let me go get dressed." I scurry off to put on some clothes and brush my teeth.

When I get back to the dining room, he's set our plates down but holds his hand out to me as he sits down. I take it with no questions until he pulls me into his lap.

"Brice, I need to eat."

"You will. I'm going to feed you." He waves a fork in my mouth with scrambled eggs on it.

I take a bite and he smiles.

"I could get used to this, you know," he says. "While I don't enjoy waking up alone, I do like finding you working in my shirt, being able to take care of you, and feeding you."

"I like being here. It's so relaxing. And I enjoy you taking care of me, too."

It's so different from my parents, or my assistant making sure I'm eating and taking care of myself. When Brice does it, it's because he cares, not because I'm his daughter or because I'm paying him a salary.

After breakfast, I help with the dishes, and he's smiling the entire time until someone knocks on his door. I jump up to answer it.

"Who the heck is that?" he grumbles.

"Don't get mad. I did something for you," I say as I walk backward toward the door.

"What did you do?"

I open the door and smile at the man on the other side. "You must be Josh."

"Yes. Kayla?"

"That's me, and this is Brice." I introduce.

"What did you do?" Brice asks again but is firmer this time.

"Well, I wanted to find a way to thank you for taking me in when I was hurt and for putting up with me recently. I noticed some things that needed to be done around here and I know you're busy at the clinic. So, I texted Sage, and she recommended Josh here to do some stuff around the house. I'm paying him, he's starting with the roof, and you will not tell me no."

He says nothing, so I continue, "Sage said Josh is her brother Mac's friend from the local Indian reservation and could use the work. She said he works on a construction crew and helped with the barn repairs as well at Mike and Lilly's place."

"Okay. Thank you, Josh." Brice forces a smile.

Josh goes to get to work on the roof, but I doubt I've heard the end of this. When I close the door and turn back to Brice, he is right behind me.

"Why did you do this?" he asks.

Though he's close enough to touch, he isn't touching me. "Because I wanted to. I know the last few days with me weren't easy, and this is my way of making up for it."

"That's not how this works. We have good days and bad days, but you're setting a dangerous precedent if you're going to do something like this every time we have a bad day." He grips my waist and pulls me to him.

"I'm okay with that. Do you want to come with me to meet with Jason and Nick tomorrow? I'm waiting on a few things to put my pitch together. I'm sure we can find something to do until it comes in." I run my hands under his shirt and up to his hard chest and washboard abs.

"I have a few dirty ideas," he whispers against my lips.

"I really like your dirty ideas."

· · · ● · ● · ● · · ·

Brice

While I have no interest in business meetings, I'm really excited to see Kayla in action today when we meet with Jason and Nick. Instead of the formal business attire she wore to the last meeting, she's in jeans and cowboy boots. She's prepared and relaxed, but even more so, she's such a different version than the woman I treated that day in my clinic.

Walking into WJ's, she is calm and confident. Jason and Nick are ready for the meeting, but they still seem hesitant. I know they're doing this for me, a fact I don't take lightly, but I know Kayla is going to rock this.

"We still don't want to franchise," Nick says as we all sit down at a table.

WJ's isn't open, so we have the place to ourselves. It has a different vibe without everyone here.

"I know. I have a better idea." Kayla pulls out the folder she has with her.

"Well, color me intrigued," Nick says, making Kayla pause.

"My grandpa used to say that when my dad told him he had a business idea," Kayla says, then shakes it off.

"Mine, too," Nick says, smiling.

"Okay, I don't want to waste your time. Brice and I were in here the other night for dinner, the night you did that BBQ brisket, which was the best brisket I've ever had by the way."

Nick gives her a genuine smile.

"I don't remember the last time I ate so much. The place smelled amazing the moment you walked in. After we ate, Brice asked me to dance. I promise I have a point, boys," Kayla says the moment she sees she might be losing them.

It's obvious to me that she's great at reading people and doing what she does.

"While we were dancing, we overheard a gentleman say he wished he could buy a bottle of the BBQ sauce to take home with him. It got my wheels turning. My dad often says sometimes you have to shift gears for the better of the company you're working with. So, I'm shifting gears."

She starts pulling out some papers with charts and numbers and places them on the table in front of Jason and Nick.

"Let's bottle your BBQ sauce and sell it. Your logo, your brand, you retain the rights, we just help you produce it. You can sell it here, but we can also start to get it on local grocery store shelves and branch out. We can do a different version of BBQ sauce, but we don't have to stop there. Whatever you do differently with your corn muffins, they're delicious. We could make a mix people can take home. Remember now, you would have full creative control. You can test items and perfect them before they go up for sale, and we only promote the products you want."

Jason and Nick look at each other, then sit up and look at the numbers in front of them.

"This isn't the first time we've done this, and we have the facilities to produce and help advertise as needed. We could do merch too-- shirts, hats, bumper stickers with a cute saying. That's a great form of advertisement. Think about this. Someone sees another person wearing a WJ's shirt, then at the store they see a WJ's product and pick it up to try it at home. They love it, and then realize when they're visiting great aunt Sally next month which is only an hour away from WJ's, so they swing in. It's all connected."

They go over some numbers, costs, projections, and ideas.

"You really think this is worth your time?" Jason asks.

"Yeah, I do. It's all about branding. It's perfect because there's already a buzz about you all the way to Dallas, and it's something we can capitalize on. Sell people on the idea of taking a piece of WJ's home with them to continue the experience. We start small between here and Dallas. As we grow, we stick to Texas, and then expand from there."

When they start talking about a number of ideas, I zone out because the business end of things isn't really my cup of tea. But Kayla is right at home. She is good at what she does, and she's patient with answering questions, even if they've been asked before.

There is a break at one point when Nick makes us some lunch–his BBQ tacos.

"I swear, if I keep eating here, I'm going to gain a hundred pounds. I've yet to have something from you that I don't like," Kayla says appreciatively.

"You'd be surprised how many people say that," Jason says.

"Do you plan to enter the BBQ competition this summer?" Kayla asks him.

"Yeah, I have to go defend my title. I was asked to do a show on the Food Network, but I had to turn it down."

"What? Why? Whatever they were offering, I can get you a better deal." Kayla kicks back into work mode.

"No, it wasn't that. It's just they aren't filming until this fall and, well, this isn't public news yet, but Maggie is pregnant and will be due around then."

"Oh, my gosh, Nick! That's exciting! Congratulations," Kayla says.

"We talked about it, and with Sage and Sarah both due this summer, the timing just wasn't right," Nick says.

There is a hint of disappointment in his eyes, and I know he wanted to do it, but family comes first. Of course, Kayla picks up on his disappointment, too.

"You wanted to do it," Kayla states.

"Yeah, if I'm being honest."

"What did you tell them when you declined?"

"The truth. My wife would be due any day and I couldn't risk missing it."

"I wouldn't be surprised if they contact you again. You didn't blow them off, you showed them you value family. They'll be contacting you again. I can almost guarantee it," she winks.

After her presentation, we finish our lunches.

"Listen, we like the idea, but we need to take it home, talk to our wives, and our family," Jason says as we start to wrap up.

"Of course! All this info is yours and my number is on the folder if you or they have questions. Call or text any time."

Once in the car, Kayla lets out the cutest little squeal.

"I don't know why that felt so good, but that meeting was so different from the ones I'm usually in. It was...I don't know. If I say it was 'human,' would that make sense?"

"Yeah, Business meetings are boring, stuffy, and more like a chess match than two people talking about a deal."

"Exactly. That's it exactly. I hate dealing with those kinds of people. But this, I enjoyed. I want more of this working with everyday people."

"So, make a shift. You can delegate out anything you don't want to do. That's the joy of being CEO."

"I think you're right," she says as we head home, and I can already see the wheels turning.

Chapter 18
Kayla

We're cuddling on the couch that night after I met with Jason and Nick at WJ's, and my mind is whirling. That meeting was the first one in years I actually enjoyed, and to me, that means I need to make a change. Brice is right. I can delegate things, so I think I want to make a change in the clients I deal with and the ones I hand off to my team.

I want to work with people on a more personal level and become more involved like I have been for WJ's.

I'm thinking of developing a new department that works with local businesses like WJ's and I want to be the one to oversee it. Without a doubt, I know I'd have dad's support. It's just the logistics that need to be worked out. It's what's been on my mind the whole time we've been watching this movie, and I have no idea what's happened. Brice is running a hand through my hair and it's the most relaxing feeling in the world.

"What are you thinking about so hard over there?" Brice's voice breaks through my thoughts.

I realize the movie has ended.

"I have this idea running around my head of starting a new department to work with local businesses like WJ's. But I want to be the one to do it. To be out there talking to these businesses."

"You did really well today. I was so proud of you, the way you had things planned, but you tailored it to them. The way you shifted focus based on what they wanted." He kisses the top of my head, sending a rash of shivers down my back.

"Actually, it was fun. For the first time in years, I enjoyed a business meeting. It won't make us a ton of money, but it will help real everyday people, and I want to be a part of that."

"So do it."

"I plan to."

"If I put on another movie, will you actually watch it?"

"No promises."

"That's what I thought. I'm putting on that new spy movie."

We snuggle back on the couch, and he watches the movie while my mind whirls and then comes to a crashing halt. I want to develop this new department and work with local companies, but all this requires that I go back to Dallas. Unfortunately, I no longer have a reason to stay for work, which means I have to get back to the office, in Dallas, almost two hours away from Brice.

I knew at some point this was going to happen, but I just kept pushing it out of my head and I never really gave it a second thought. Now I have no game plan. I can stay a few more days, but I need to be back at the office by Monday.

So instead of thinking about the new department or my next steps at work, I'm finally thinking of my next steps with Brice.

"Have you ever thought of living anywhere else?" I ask almost without thinking.

I know we've talked about it before, but my head needs to hear it again.

"No. My family, friends, practice, and home are here. I have no desire to live anywhere else."

"You could make a lot more money in Dallas."

With those words, his whole body goes stiff.

"It isn't about the money. This town is my home and I love it here. I went away for school, and I was miserable and hated every minute of it. First chance I had to come home, I took it."

I nod, but I guess part of me was hoping maybe he'd change his mind and make things easier on me. On us.

"Where is all this coming from?" he asks, not moving or even turning to look at me.

Here is the talk I've been putting off but we're now at the point where we don't have a choice.

"Well, I need to go back to Dallas because I have to get back to work. I did what I came out here to do, and if I'm going to open this new department, I have to be in Dallas, at the company, to do it."

His hands stop moving and we both barely breathe. We know what this means. Our perfect little bubble is broken.

"So where does that leave us?" he finally asks the question neither of us wanted to voice.

I don't have an answer. His life is here in Rock Springs, and mine is in Dallas. Outside of building a magical transportation device, the answer is simply, I don't know. Though I don't have a long-term answer, I might have a short-term one.

"In two weeks, I have a charity gala. It's for cancer research, the type my grandfather died from. Come with me as my date. See a different side of my life and meet my friends?"

His whole body relaxes, and he finally turns to look at me.

"I'd really like that. I don't know how this is going to work, but I don't want it to end."

He leans in and places a kiss softly on my lips.

"I don't want this to end, either. We can talk every day, text all day, video call at night."

"I like how you think. When do you have to leave?"

"Sunday night. I need to be back at work on Monday."

"We have three days, and I plan to spend them in bed with you, reminding you of all the reasons you're mine."

Chapter 19

Brice

It's been two of the longest weeks of my life. Being away from Kayla physically hurts, and I hate every minute of it. She calls me every morning and we talk while we both get ready for work. Then we text all day, sometimes sneaking away for a lunchtime phone call. Every night from the moment she gets home until we both go to sleep, we video chat.

Many nights those video calls turn very dirty because the need in me to remind her she's mine is strong. Though she's beautiful and successful and could have any guy in Dallas she wants, she picks me. While I know she wants me, part of me worries she will tire of the long-distance because no matter how hard we try, neither of us has a long-term plan.

Last weekend, my dad, who loved being back at the clinic, took over for me so I could spend the weekend with Kayla. I needed to hold her in my arms because sleeping without her has become nearly impossible. That weekend we both caught up on much-needed sleep between rounds of love-making. We didn't leave her apartment, much less her bed.

Now I'm back in Dallas. I got in last night and am getting ready for the gala event. I'm not thrilled about having to ditch my cowboy boots and wear a suit, but I know how important this is for her. I have to say, a real perk of staying in Kayla's Dallas Penthouse is the bathroom space. We're both able to easily get ready for this event. The bonus is, I can watch her get ready in person instead of on the phone like I've been doing each morning.

She is in a stunning deep green dress that makes her hair and eyes pop. It's tight at the waist and flows loosely around her legs. All I can think about is if she's wearing anything underneath it. When I ask her, she just smirks, which doesn't help my thoughts much.

I attempt to focus on something else, like how I would decorate this place if I lived here with her because even though she says she has lived here for over three years, the place doesn't have much style. There's only one painting on the wall in the living room and nothing on any of the walls throughout the rest of the place. There is the essential furniture, a few photos, and that's it.

If it weren't for the photos, there would be no way to tell who lives here. There is no personality. Heck, it looks more like a bachelor pad than the home of a kick ass female CEO. I asked her about it last night. She says her dad picked this place out for its security, but it has never really felt like home. She commented that my house feels more like home to her than her place. Which made me want to ask her to move in with me. Though the timing was wrong and I'm sure that wouldn't work, so I just made love to her until we both passed out.

I've been standing here watching her, and she catches my eye in the mirror.

"I'm ready when you are," she says.

"I could stand here and watch you all night. But let's get this over with so we can get back here, and I can peel that dress off you and see what you do or don't have under it."

Smirking at me again, she takes my hand as we head downstairs. "I got a car for us today, so we don't have to deal with traffic or worry about having a drink or two."

Even though this is a smart idea, I wouldn't have minded driving us.

I let her slide into the back seat first and then follow her in. When the door closes, she leans in and gives me a chaste kiss.

"You look really handsome, and the women tonight will just eat you up, but I prefer you in what you wore to Ford's wedding."

I swear I know right then and there I'm in love with this woman, and it couldn't be a worse time to tell her. Until we figure this out, I can't tell her, or else I just risk hurting us both even more.

When we arrive, there is a line of cars waiting to drop people off.

My nerves suddenly kick in. "You didn't say there would be photos and a red carpet." "I know. I didn't want to make you even more nervous. But I swear you don't have to do anything but smile, because I'll handle any questions, okay? It's a big event. Anyone who is anyone in Dallas Society is going to be here and the governor is even making an appearance."

It's becoming clear the number of things I'll do for this woman and if she only knew, it could be very dangerous. I'll gladly stand by her side and smile for photos because it will let everyone know she is mine, and I'm hers. Though I better give my mom a heads up about the photos because she'll be wanting to get some printed and share them around town.

Pulling out my phone, I shoot my mom a quick text.

"Can't let your mother get scooped on the gossip?" she chuckles.

Already she knows me, my family, and even Rock Springs so well. So, I just nod, send the text, and mute my phone for the night.

When it's our turn, my nerves kick into full gear but one look at her and everything feels right.

Here goes nothing.

The driver opens the door and I step out, ignoring the cameras, and turning to offer Kayla a hand. She takes it and before her foot even hits the pavement flashes are going off, people are yelling questions, and security is fighting to keep people back. I don't pay attention to any of it, simply focusing on Kayla and keeping her eyes on me as she steps out of the car.

She tucks her arm in mine, and we make our way up the red carpet. She stops and poses a few times for photos and answers a few work--related questions but ignores anything about me, or us, or her time away from the office.

The moment we are inside, I almost sag with relief.

"I don't know how you do that," I tell her.

"Since I was raised in this life, it's almost second nature. Doesn't mean I like it. Just means I know how to deal with it."

That's when her parents walk up.

"We were watching, and you handled that well," her dad says, shaking my hand. It's all very public and I'm sure it's a sign of his approval of me or something like that. It's very apparent that at an event like this a man of his status does nothing just because.

Kayla keeps her hand in mine as we circulate and start talking to other couples. She introduces me, and other than a polite hello and nice to meet you, they are more interested in talking to Kayla, which is fine by me. I'm more than happy to focus my attention on her as well.

It isn't until a group of women walks up to us that things change.

"Kayla! You have missed too many brunches. Next weekend you can't skip out on us again."

Kayla laughs and hugs each of the four women.

"Girls, this is Brice. He's a doctor. Brice these are my friends, Ava, Kelsey, Beth, and Willa."

"Nice to meet you," I tell them.

Kayla chats with them for a minute, assuring them she was out of town and not just ditching them. But the whole time they keep eyeing me as if I'm a prime steak they plan to eat for dinner.

When a gentleman I remember seeing at her office but can't recall his name steps up to introduce her to someone else, the woman turns to me.

"So, where do you practice?" the redhead asks—Willa, I think.

"I have my own practice in Rock Springs."

"You look young to have your own place," Ava says.

"Well, I took it over from my father when he retired."

"Where is Rock Springs?" Willa asks.

"It's a small town west of here."

"Small town? Why don't you get a job here in Dallas where most people really are?"

"Stop, Willa. Not everyone is cut out to be a big city doctor. He took over from his father, after all," Ava says.

I stand there in complete shock at how openly rude these women are.

"So, why are you here with Kayla? Do you have something to do with the charity?" Beth asks.

"No, I'm her date," I say.

"Yes, but why?" Willa asks.

I don't even have an answer to that question. If there was a reason, it would be that Kayla would only bring me as a date. But apparently, in these women's minds, there can't be any possible way we are dating.

"You'd have to ask her," I say as they stare me down.

When Kayla comes back, they're all smiles, like we were getting along perfectly.

I, on the other hand, am ready to go, and we haven't even had dinner yet. Thankfully, we make our way to the table and none of the girls we just met are there.

The woman next to me at dinner seems to have the same mindset as Kayla's friends. Why would I want to practice in a small town instead of Dallas? Why did Kayla bring me tonight? How could we have possibly met? Have I met her parents?

With every fiber of being, I try to grin and bear it because I know how important this night is for her. But she can sense something is wrong and pulls me to the side.

"Thank you for tonight. I just need to talk to the Governor and then we can go," she says.

I nod and watch her talk with him from the sidelines.

Kayla's mom walks up beside me. "You're doing better than I did at my first event."

"I'm not going to lie, these aren't people I want to spend time with."

"Oh, dear, neither do we. But they are people that are better on your side and in your back pocket in case you need them than to have them against you. It's a chess game. Tiring but necessary."

She squeezes my arm and rejoins her husband as Kayla walks up.

"I called the car. Are you ready to leave?"

"Yep."

We head out and on the car ride home she talks about this person, or that one who said this or that, and the entire way her mom's words are stuck in my head.

This is Kayla's world. She has to interact with these people, and will always be going to events like this. But her friends? Is this how they act? Those are the people she chooses to keep around her. Is she like that and I just missed it? But that doesn't seem possible. My Kayla is nothing like those women. She's sweet, loving, and cares deeply about people.

Look what she did for the illegal rodeo, putting her name on the line to do the right thing. She helped Bill and didn't want people to know it was her. She isn't like them, yet she has to be like them to a degree to call them friends.

The more I think about it, the more I know this just isn't going to work. I'm never going to be okay with events like this and being treated in this manner. It's obvious I'm never going to be comfortable here and there is no way in hell I will ever move to this city. But Kayla's company is here, so this is where she has to be.

When we get back to her place, I start packing my bag, as there is no point in putting this off.

"What are you doing?" She places her hand on mine to stop me.

"I can't be part of this life."

"Brice, you haven't given it a chance."

"My friends went out of their way to make you feel welcome even though the only reason you were in town was to try to convince their brother to do something he didn't want to do. Did they not?"

"Of course, they did. I had a great time at the BBQ and the wedding."

"Your friends went out of their way to show me I don't belong."

She shakes her head. "They didn't, they were nice to you."

"They were nice around you. When you stepped away, they wanted to know why you brought me. Was I attached to the charity? They made it clear I couldn't be a good doctor because I chose to practice in a small town and took over my father's practice."

"You must have misunderstood them. Sometimes they twist their words."

"I find that hard to believe for people of their status in your world. What kind of life do you really want, Kayla?"

She opens her mouth and closes it several times, but doesn't speak.

"You know what kind of life I want? I want to go to sleep beside the woman I love every night. I want to wake up with her in my arms or find her working in the kitchen with her hair pulled up in a messy bun and wearing nothing but my shirt. When I get emergency phone calls, I want her by my side, comforting the family when I can't. Knowing she has my back. I want to watch her give my mom as good as she gets. I want you, Kayla. I want what we had back in Rock Springs, around people that care and that are genuine and nice. I love you, and I want you, but not here, not like this."

I finish packing my bag and turn to find her parents standing there with shock on their faces.

"You...umm. You left your jacket, Kayla. We wanted to bring it to you with the cold front coming in," her mom says.

"It was nice to meet you both. Thank you for being nice to me, though I'm sure I'm the last person you wanted your daughter with." With that, I walk straight to my truck and go home.

Chapter 20

Kayla

"Dammit!"

Jen, my assistant peeks her head in.

"Girl, you just need to go home and eat your feelings over whatever is going on and cry yourself to sleep," she says when I yell at my computer for the tenth time today.

I'm so distracted, I keep making stupid mistakes. Never have I been this off my game.

"Seriously, you should go. The Board is starting to notice. Go home. Get your head on straight. I can redirect them by gossiping about this illegal rodeo you helped shut down. It's still the talk all over town. Some big developer is trying to make all sorts of deals now."

Crap, if the Board has noticed, then she's right. I need to get my head back in the game. Jen can distract them and I know she's right.

"Okay, I'll see you tomorrow, maybe."

"I know we aren't close, but do you need to talk about it?" she asks with such sincerity in her eyes that I break down and have her come into my office and lock the door.

I pour her a drink and launch into the story from my first meeting at WJ's to my accident, meeting Brice, staying with him, the people of

Rock Springs, my time with Brice, my second meeting at WJ's, the busting of the illegal rodeo, the long-distance, the gala, the fight, and Brice's I love you bomb, ending with my fight with Ava, Kelsey, Beth, and Willa on Monday.

When I'm done, she stands up and pours herself another drink, and chugs it.

"Damn, how are you even out of bed?"

"I have a company to run. Plus, I'm not even sleeping in my own bed."

"This world isn't going to change. The people around you aren't going to change. You need to decide what you want, and the only thing you can change is you and your location. You're good, no scratch that. You're fucking amazing at your job. I'm one of many women who look up to you, but this job isn't worth giving up your happiness and or your life. No job is. This job isn't going to keep you warm at night and be there when you're sick."

Jen's right. I know she is. She's not saying anything I haven't thought, even if I try to push those thoughts away.

"What I haven't heard is how you feel about him. That is what you need to figure out. Once you do, then the rest will be easy."

"You're right. I'll go home and try to get my head on straight."

"Just shoot me a text if you aren't coming in. I've got your back."

"Thanks."

I stop and get take out on my way home. But the moment I step in the door, it's like every night. Brice is here and I see him in every corner of the place. I can't even sleep in my bed. I've been sleeping in the guest room. The one-room he was never in.

I change into my lounge clothes and sit down to eat. I've been seeing the people around me in a new light and I'm not liking what I see.

Bright and early Monday morning, Ava, Kelsey, Beth, and Willa marched into my office and dragged me to lunch. What Brice had said was still fresh in my head so when Willa asked what I was thinking by bringing him to the event and then they all burst out giggling...well, I felt no shame in tossing my water in her face, calling them all insensitive bitches, and telling them to lose my number before stomping out.

Everything Brice had told me was true, and I just blew him off about all of it. It forced me to look at everyone around me with new eyes. And honestly, I hated what I saw. I was appalled when I started comparing them to how the people in Rock Springs treated me. It was a night and day difference.

I tried to watch some TV, but my mind was on Brice, on that last night when I should have taken his side but didn't, and how badly I screwed things up.

"Goodness, dear, didn't you hear us knocking?"

Mom walks in and turns the TV off.

"No. Sorry, my head is elsewhere."

"We heard you went home early and wanted to check on you."

"Brice was right. About what Ava, Kelsey, Beth, and Willa said to him. They confirmed it at lunch on Monday. I may have thrown water in Willa's face and told them off before storming out."

"Lucky for you, it didn't make the papers," Mom says, scolding me.

"I'm starting to see everyone around me through new eyes, and I hate it. My head isn't in the game, and I don't know how to fix it." I toss my head back on the couch and look up at my ceiling.

"Sweetheart. You can be a CEO from anywhere, but you can't be Brice's wife from Dallas," Dad says.

I jerk my head up to look at him. "What?"

"You can do eighty percent of your work from home. What you have to do in the office, you can. You have the money to buy a helicopter, and Brice has the land. There is a helipad on the roof of the office. You can be in the office in forty-five minutes tops and back home for dinner that night when you have to be here."

My head is spinning as I stare at my father.

"You guys have always lived in the city."

"Because we loved it. I enjoy doing lunches and helping charities, and you loved your private school. It made sense for us. But it doesn't mean it has to make sense for you," Mom says.

Why hadn't this crossed my mind? This whole time I've been sitting here thinking my entire life is in Dallas, and that it has to be. This opens up so many more possibilities, but at the same time, still a lot to decide.

"Wait, when did we get a helicopter pad on the roof of the office?"

"When I was making trips to a business in Fort Worth and kept getting stuck for hours in traffic. I rented a helicopter for a few months and then decided to buy one and put in the pad. It saved me hours in traffic," Dad says.

"I didn't know that."

"Well, you have a lot to think about. Just know we want you happy. We like Brice, and if you being happy means moving to Rock Springs, we support you. If it means being here, then we support that. If being happy means stepping down as CEO, I'll support that, too, okay? You're my daughter first and always. Everything else is secondary," Dad says.

I stand up to hug him and don't even bother hiding the tears. Mom hugs me from behind, and knowing I have their support makes things a lot easier, even if I still don't know what I'm going to do just yet.

After Mom and Dad leave, I take the food downstairs to Walter. He opens the door and takes one look at me in my sweats, and shakes his head.

"Man problems, work problems, or family problems?"

"All three? I bought dessert, too." I hold up some of the cake my chef left me as well.

"Alright. I'll eat you talk."

And I do. Just like with my assistant, I tell him everything, including what my parents told me. Then I sit back and watch his wheels turn.

"When I met my wife, we had a bit of a whirlwind like you. We had issues we had to sort out, and it wasn't easy, but we made it work. Even after we were married, there were tough times. I'd give anything for one more day with her, even if it was a day full of fighting. Don't look back and wish you hadn't wasted time."

"Why is everything you always tell me so damn cryptic?"

"Because people need to come to their own decisions, but for you, I'll make an exception. You already know in your heart what you want to do. You're just looking for someone to tell you it's okay. Someone other than your parents. Well, I'm telling you. It's okay to choose Brice, to work from Rock Springs. It's okay to get a helicopter or quit being CEO. Just leap."

"What if it doesn't work out?"

"You wouldn't be this torn up if it wasn't serious. If it doesn't work, you have options. Come back to Dallas. I'm sure your parents would be happy to have you, and if not, you can sleep on my couch for a bit. You can do this. And I expect a formal invitation to the wedding."

I laugh then because all the stress and tension are gone.

"If this works out, I'll send a car to come get you and have you out there for the weekend. Talk about writing inspiration. It's like something out of a romance book. The little old ladies there will eat you alive."

"I'll hold you to that. Now, tell me about your time in Rock Springs."

I spend the next two hours laughing and telling him all about my visit, the church ladies, the wedding, and the illegal rodeo bust. All of it.

"This sounds like the kind of place that is worth leaving Dallas for," he agrees when we're done.

"I completely agree."

"Well, it sounds like you have some planning and packing to do, so go get to it. Make sure you come to say goodbye before you head out of town."

"I'm going to keep my chef on, but have her start coming here and making meals for you. It will give me peace of mind knowing you're eating."

"Can I tell her what meals I like?"

"Of course. She made that chocolate cake."

"Deal. Now get going."

I go up to my apartment and for the first time in days, I'm happy to be there. The memories of Brice don't make me sad.

I pull out my laptop and get to work on getting things in order. I have a lot to do if I'm going to prove that I'm all in. But I just hope I'm not too late.

When I crawl into bed that night, it's into my own bed. Though I swear I can still smell Brice in it. It's the best night's sleep I can remember ever getting.

The next day, I start making calls and let my parents know of my decision. They show me nothing but love and support. My dad helps me set up a meeting with the board members and promises to stand by my side when I tell them my plans. They could say no, but really, they're just a formality. Between my dad and me, we still own over fifty percent of the company stocks.

I have a few moments of doubt about my choices, but sometimes when you finally make a hard choice, the universe has a way of telling you that you're on the right path. So, when my phone goes off and I get that confirmation, there is no going back.

Chapter 21

Brice

I'm at my parent's place and working on the pigpen my mom wants. She's been hinting at a pen to raise some baby pigs and I need the distraction, so it works out. I try to keep Kayla out of my head, and the harder I work, the easier that seems to be. The harder the work, and the more tired I am at night, the easier it is to fall asleep. Though really, trying to fall asleep without her is very difficult, if not impossible.

I've already pulled weeds all around my place, the clinic, and my parent's place, fixed a few stalls in my parent's barn, organized all the files in the clinic, and changed the oil in my truck, as well as my parents' cars. Nothing seems to be enough to get her off my mind. But all I need is time, right? Keep busy and eventually, it will get easier.

I told my parents what happened. They say some time apart is probably what we need, but my dad admitted he wouldn't have left. He said it's the equivalent of going to bed mad. You just don't do it. I understand, but I just didn't see a solution.

Over the last few days, I have considered moving to Dallas many times. For her I would, but I know I'd be miserable, and that would seep into the relationship as much as I'd try to prevent it from happening. Not to mention there is no way I can hang around those people at the gala and bite my tongue again. Next time, I'll tell them exactly what they can do with their opinions, and that will probably make the front page of every Dallas paper.

So that leaves me right back here. Working to forget about Kayla, which isn't helping, but at least things around here are getting done. I think my mom is enjoying this because she made me a to-do list around the house of all the things my dad hasn't gotten to yet, including repainting the house.

I'm so focused on the to-do list, I don't hear anyone walking up to me until I turn and find Sage and Colt standing there. They just watch me, but I can tell they know exactly what's going on. If my mom didn't tell them when they got here, I'm sure the gossip tree knows by now.

"I'm going to go have some tea on the porch with your mom," Colt says before squeezing Sage's hand and kissing her cheek.

We both watch him walk up to the back porch where Mom meets him with a tray of drinks and I'm sure a snack of some kind.

"Did you draw the short straw?" I ask Sage.

"No, I volunteered to come talk to you."

Sage was the girl I had a crush on in school, but everyone knew she and Colt were thick as thieves even if no one knew for sure they were together. A few years back, Sage asked me out, and I jumped at the chance. What guy doesn't want a date with the girl he crushed on all through school? But it was clear from that first date we were better off as friends.

We talked a lot, and she shared what was going on with her and Colt at the time. After some brainstorming, we decided to go on a few more dates to see if we could get him to finally make a move. It worked exactly as we had hoped it would. They have been together ever since. When Colt took Sage down memory lane with a scavenger hunt around town before he proposed, he asked me to be a part of it.

Sage takes a seat on the stack of wood I've been using to build the pen. "Why don't you tell me what happened so I'm not going off what the town gossips have filled in?" I can only imagine what the town gossips know, and what details they're making up. So, I launch into the story of Kayla having to go back to work and the long-distance we did and the gala, her friends, what they said, and our fight after I told her I loved her, her lack of reaction, her parents seeing it all, and me leaving.

"I feel like I need a bottle of whiskey after that," Sage jokes but rubs her stomach.

She looks back over at Colt, who hasn't taken his eyes off her. She smiles at him and he smiles back at her. I want that, what they have with each other. I've watched each of her brothers find it and many other couples here in Rock Springs, including my best friend, Ford. Until I met Kayla, I was thinking it just wasn't on the cards for me. But the universe is a cruel bitch and ardently likes toying with people.

"Listen," Sage says. "After school, I left and traveled a lot. I experienced many different lifestyles and ways of living. I saw people who were obvious soul mates and some in miserable marriages. Even though I was trying to find where I fit, the problem was, I already knew. I was just scared of the answer. I spent many days asking for a sign of what I should do. When my family's ranch went up for sale, it was the sign I needed to come home."

Sage's birth parents were very abusive. Blaze and his family lived next door to them, and Sage and Blaze became best friends. So, when he went to his mom for help after finding out what was happening with Sage, they took her in, no questions asked, and ended up adopting her into the family. A few years later Colt needed a home, and they took him in, too. But by then I'm sure there was already something between Sage and Colt, even if they didn't know what it was right then.

"But I know Rock Springs is where I'm meant to be. I was miserable in Dallas," I say. "I miss Kayla so damn much, I've thought of giving all this up and moving there for her. Yet I know within five years it would destroy us. If I lasted that long. I couldn't even handle a weekend there, or even one event."

Sage smiles, looking back over at Colt again. "You know what you want, just like Colt did. But Kayla is like me. She's going to need some time to figure it out. Thinking about making so many changes in her life, well, it's a lot. Don't forget she has a company to worry about, too. But she needs help and a reminder of what she has here. Though Colt let me have my space, I often wonder if I would have come home sooner if he hadn't. If we had kept talking, things would have been so much easier and we wouldn't have lost so much time. Anyway, just something to think about."

"I don't know what to even say. We had that huge fight and her parents saw it all..."

"You're overthinking this. A simple 'I miss you' text can go a long way. Photos are even better, just no dick pics, okay?"

"So what you're telling me is if Colt had sent you a dick pic you wouldn't have beelined home to take a ride?"

"Brice!"

Her face turns bright red. To this day, one of my favorite things to do is embarrass Sage and get her to turn as red a tomato. It takes a lot to get to Sage, but when you can, it's fun as hell.

Sage yelling my name causes Colt to come our way and I just chuckle.

"Colt, I'm sorry for the inappropriate thing I said to your wife, but in all fairness, she started it."

He takes one look at Sage's still red face and smirks. "What did you do?"

"She brought up dick pics," I shrug.

"Now you've done it," she says.

"You don't need dick pics, my wife. You can see the real thing in person at any time. Now that you've gotten real up close and personal with him, let's go." Colt growls the last part.

"Thanks a lot, Brice. If I wasn't already pregnant, I for sure would be after today!"

The entire time Colt is dragging her back to his truck, I belly laugh. I know I'll have to formally apologize to the two of them later, but right now all I want is to have a cold beer with my best friend. So, I go back to my place and avoid the dagger eyes from my mom, who I'm sure has plenty of questions about what just happened. I wash up and go over to Ford's place.

When I hit the gate I hesitate, since he's married now, and I don't know the rule of just dropping by like I used to. Sure as hell, I won't be letting myself into the house as I used to do. God knows what I might walk in on.

I'm already here, so it can't hurt to go knock on the door. Savannah answers with a big smile.

"Brice! Did I know you were coming over?" She greets me with a hug and another smile before stepping to the side and letting me in.

"Not unless you're a mind reader. I'm sorry I didn't think about calling until I was already at the gate."

"Nonsense, you're always welcome. At least you knocked, Lilly still refuses to."

I laugh. "One day your sister will walk in on something she doesn't want to see and then she will always knock."

"I doubt it. Ford is down at the barn. We just had the cutest little horse born this morning. Please tell me you'll stay for dinner. I've cooked enough for twenty."

"I'd like that."

"Okay, now off with you. Tell Ford dinner is in an hour."

Going out the back door to the barn, I find Ford with one of the ranch hands leaning over a stall. As I walk up, he turns to greet me.

"Hey, check out this little guy," he says as the ranch hand leaves to give us some privacy.

In the stall are the foal and his mother. The little guy is walking around on wobbly legs, and I know this is a moment I want to share with

Kayla. So, I take out my phone and take a few photos and even a video of the foal trying to walk. But then I hesitate and don't send them. With a sigh, I tuck my phone back into my pocket.

"Come on, I have some beers in the office, and you can tell me what's on your mind," Ford says.

"That obvious?"

"That, and your mom called when you left the house and figured you were heading this way."

Following Ford to the office he has set up in the barn, I sit on the leather couch and take the beer he offers. Then in the interest of not wasting his time, I tell him everything, down to Sage's conversation and my dick pic comments which have him rolling.

"I'm surprised Colt didn't punch you."

"Yeah, me too." I take the last swig of my beer, and Ford is right there to replace it.

"You probably don't want to hear it, but I agree with Sage about letting her know you still miss her and about avoiding the dick pics."

I pull out my phone and stare at the pictures I just took, then pick one and send it to Kayla.

Me: This little guy was just born this morning, and I was wishing you were here to share it with me.

Then I hit send and leave it be. Ford and I get to talking and then go in for dinner, but I never get a reply back from her.

I guess I have my answer. The bridge from Dallas to Rock Springs is just too big to cross.

Chapter 22

Kayla

I've never been so happy to get a photo of a baby horse, but it was the olive branch that I needed to know I was making the right choice.

As promised, my dad stood by my side with the Board and while they weren't thrilled, they were reminded they didn't have much choice. When my dad was ready to hand over his CEO responsibilities to me, he hadn't really been ready to retire so he was more than willing to take point in the Dallas office when I wasn't here. That seemed to lessen everyone's nerves and bought us at least five years to figure it out from there. Mom isn't ready for Dad to retire, which she has made clear, too. Though, they plan to do more traveling together.

The helicopter has been bought and is in storage right now and I have a guy lined up to build me a helicopter pad in Rock Springs if this all lines up. I even bought a company car to use when I'm here if needed. It will stay parked in the company parking garage.

With the company taken care of, I've been focusing on the personal side of things. Packing, listing my penthouse, which sold remarkably fast. I guess the building had a waitlist for people interested in it. Thank you,

Dad, for that one. When I offered to pay him back for it, he refused, and we settled on donating the money to charity. It was a win-win.

Walter is over the moon to have the chef come in. He's already given her his list of demands as he calls it, but really, it's just his favorite foods. She's thrilled to work with him and said he reminds her of her own grandfather who she lost a few years back.

Before I go, I head down to check on Walter one more time.

I knock on the door and wait for him.

"Kayla, the door is open. Why do you even bother knocking?" he hollers from the other side.

I laugh and let myself in. He's at his desk typing away. So I wait until he reaches a spot where he can take a break. Once, when I interrupted him, I got an earful, and a guilt trip for a week because he lost his spot. Needless to say, I learned my lesson.

"You're getting ready to head out?" he asks, spinning around in his chair.

"Yes, there is just one more thing we need to take care of," I tell him.

He eyes me suspiciously. "What's that?"

"Let me see your phone."

He hands it over but watches every move I make.

I download the car service app and log into the account I set up for him.

"This is the car service app I was telling you about."

We had talked about this last week. He really shouldn't be driving anymore, and I don't want to worry about him when I'm not here. We argued then and I know we'll argue now.

"Ahh, why can't I just have the doorman call me a taxi?"

"This is much safer. And they will help with your bags, groceries, and even pick up takeout and bring it to you."

"Why are you doing this Kayla?" he asks, leaning back in his chair.

I tear up because I'm going to miss him like crazy.

"Outside my parents, you are the one person who tells me like it is. You don't sugarcoat anything, and you don't want anything from me. You have helped make my company millions of dollars and wanted nothing in return. When I needed it, you have kept me company and are just an all-around good person. Making this choice to go after Brice was easy, and leaving Dallas and my so-called friends was easy. The only thing I'm struggling with is leaving you."

He turns his head and looks out the window, but I swear his eyes are covered in the same mist as mine are.

"I love my grandkids, but they don't want anything to do with me. They are more worried about dyeing their hair purple, their next body piercing, and their next boyfriend. You're the family I wish I had. I expect an invitation to dinner as soon as you get settled."

"I'll even let you come in on the helicopter."

A huge smile takes over his face, and I know I got him there. "I'm going to hold you to it."

We say our goodbyes with a few tearful hugs. Once I'm back in my penthouse I call down for one of the desk guys to help me with loading some boxes into my car. The rest of the stuff is divided into piles to donate or will come with me to Rock Springs or end up in storage, depending on how this goes. My mom promised to take care of this for me. When I know.

Taking one last look at the view of the downtown Dallas skyline that has been the best part of this apartment, I grab my bag and purse and go down to my now packed car. I sit there and stare at the text Brice sent me again. While I must have typed up at least twenty different responses, I deleted them all because none of them meant anything. My parents taught me actions speak louder than words. I'm giving him actions, not words.

Not even feeling sad about it, I get in and head out of Dallas. I cried saying goodbye to my parents this morning and even saying goodbye to Walter, but leaving Dallas? I'm not sad, it feels right, freeing. With the Dallas traffic, the drive will be just under two hours and that gives me plenty of time to figure out exactly what to say. It also gives me plenty of time for the nerves to kick in and make me doubt everything. But I've made it this far and I'm not giving up now. I'll not sit in my nursing home bed and wonder what if.

Entering Rock Springs, I decide to check the clinic first. My best guess is that's where he is and finding his truck there, I know I was right. After parking my car in the back of the parking lot, I take a few deep breaths. I've faced some of the toughest businessmen in the boardroom, made deals other companies were too scared to make, and even made grown men cry and never once blinked an eye.

Now?

Well, now I'm scared to death because I can't control this outcome. There are no stats and graphs to back me up. Matters of the heart are just so much damn harder than matters of the boardroom. Am I really banking all my hopes on one text that I still haven't managed to answer?

Just do it, Kayla.

Getting out of the car on shaky legs, I make my way into the clinic. More than ever, I'm thankful to be wearing my cowboy boots rather than heels because I'm sure I'd have fallen flat on my face by now.

There are only a couple of patients in the waiting room, and they look at me then back to their phones. Before I have a chance to ask the receptionist about Brice, his dad steps into the waiting room with a folder, most likely to call a patient back. But when he sees me, he freezes, and then a smile covers his face.

"Tell me you're here with good news and not to break my son's heart."

"Well, my car is filled with boxes, and as of tomorrow at three p.m. I'm officially homeless if today doesn't go well."

"He's in his office. You know where it is?"

I just nod. Knowing he's in the building kicks my nerves up a notch, but I hug Brice's dad before going down the hall to his office. Seeing the door is cracked open, I peek in, finding him on the computer, so I step inside and close the door behind me.

Looking up, Brice does a double take before standing, but he doesn't move.

"You were right."

"No, I...."

"No, please I've spent the last two hours in the car practicing what I was going to say, so let me get this out."

He knows, and the ghost of a smile crosses his face.

"You were right. I was so caught up in work that I didn't really notice the people around me. Mostly I think I blocked out the bad, so I didn't have to deal with it. But on Monday when I had lunch with the girls, and they said to my face what they had said to you? Well, I'm shocked it wasn't all over page sixty-one because I threw a drink in Willa's face and told them exactly what they could do with their sky-high stilettos."

I take a step closer to him.

"Then all week, I couldn't concentrate on work. I was screwing up little things, even sending the wrong emails to people. When I went home early, my dad came over and had a serious talk with me. I realized what I should have known all along–my parents will support anything I want to do. But when my dad gave me some solutions for what was holding me back, it's as if a key unlocked all sorts of possibilities. I don't know if you still love me, or even still want me, but dammit Brice, I love you, and want you."

Faster than I could have imagined, he has me in his arms and is holding me tight.

"I love you, too. So much. I still want you more than I want my next breath, but I haven't found a way to make this work. Even though

I've thought of moving to Dallas, and I really have, I know eventually I'll end up hating it so much it will ruin us."

"Well, I have a solution if you're willing to hear it?"

"Are you kidding me? Of course, I'm willing to hear it." Then he pulls me into his lap. Even though he hasn't kissed me yet, I'm more than happy that he can't keep his hands off me.

"I can do my work, most of it, anywhere. Plus, I want to head up a new division working with smaller companies like WJ's and helping them expand, and want to keep it local. So, I figured I'd only need to actually be in the office once a week. Then my dad tells me he had a helicopter pad installed on the roof of the office. Which got me thinking. It's a two-hour drive here, or more with traffic, but only about forty minutes by helicopter. Do you think you and your parents would mind me using some of the land to put in a landing pad and hanger?"

"Are you kidding?" he says, but his tone is flat and unreadable, so I push ahead.

"I already bought a car to keep at the office in case I need it. My dad will still be working, so the Dallas office is covered. My apartment is sold, movers are coming tomorrow to move my boxes either here or to storage, and my car is loaded with everything I need. I've set Walter up with my chef and a car service...." I don't get to finish my sentence because his lips are on mine.

This kiss isn't rushed, but it's like coming home. Now I finally feel like I belong.

"If building a helicopter pad means getting you here, I'm all for it. The movers better be bringing your stuff here tomorrow and if there-'s anything else you need to make this work, I'll make it happen."

"Well, I might need faster internet at the house..."

"Done."

"Also, I was thinking of opening a satellite office here in town. I'd like to keep business and work separate, especially when I have meetings. But I need to hire an assistant, someone local, so if you know anyone looking for a job, no experience needed."

His lips are on mine again, and it effectively shuts down my brain.

"Let's go home," he says, pulling me away.

"One more thing."

"Yes?"

"If this worked out, I promised Walter we'd have him out for dinner. He wants the first ride from Dallas in the helicopter."

"You could have the president out for dinner if it means you're moving in with me," he laughs.

"Thank God, because I wasn't looking forward to being homeless."

Chapter 23

Brice

Three Months Later

I never thought I'd see a day when Rock Springs had a helicopter pad. When it was unveiled, it was a huge event. By huge event, I mean my mom invited everyone out to the ranch to come see it.

As promised, Walter got the first ride out to Rock Spring for dinner. He got the royal treatment which included a tour of the town. He and Mrs. Willow hit it off and somehow, she convinced him to move out here. Kayla was so excited about it she took care of everything, and as of last week, Walter is now a Rock Springs resident.

Kayla, of course, is beyond thrilled, and they now have lunch together several times a week. She likes keeping him close and being able to keep an eye on him. When she gets stuck at work, she goes to him to talk and always walks away with new ideas.

"What are you thinking about so hard over there?" Kayla asks as we snuggle up in the bed of my truck, which I have parked in the field. We love to watch the sunset whenever we can.

"You, actually. How much happier you are with Walter here."

"I am. He was the one thing I regretted leaving in Dallas. With him here, everything is perfect."

"No regrets about your choice to move here?"

"Only one."

I stiffen because it's been a bit of a bumpy road. Kayla got the helicopter pad and hanger built as fast as she could and even has a temporary pilot. But he's made it clear it's temporary, so she's been working on getting her license. But with work, her time to get her flying hours in is limited.

"What is it?" I'm almost afraid to know.

She rolls onto her stomach and lifts her head to look at me. "That I didn't do it sooner."

Relaxing, I pull her on top of me and kiss her. I wish she had done it sooner, too, but she's here now and that is all that matters. When she pulls back, she tucks herself into my side and we curl up and watch the sunset in the beautiful Texas sky.

"So, I was talking to my dad, and while he enjoys being retired, he also misses being at the clinic. He said he doesn't want to do it full-time like when you were here, but maybe one day a week."

"I think it will be good for him and your mom. He's been driving her crazy with all the animals he wants to get. You know he bought two alpacas?"

"And Mom let him keep them?" I ask because I haven't heard this story yet.

My mom and Kayla have lunch together once a week, normally the day after she comes back from Dallas. I'm pretty sure it's so she doesn't get scooped on the latest gossip.

"Of course not. Before your dad even got home, they were sent back."

I chuckle at the story. I love how well Kayla and my mom get along even if sometimes it's to my disadvantage.

"Well, he wants to come back to the clinic one day a week. There really is no reason for the two of us to be there, so I was thinking, what if he came in on the days you go to Dallas. I'll go with you and do some volunteer work while you're at work? There's a free clinic a few blocks from your office that could use the help."

"I love the idea. It means more time with you. And whatever you need for the clinic, you let me know. I'll make it happen."

"I know you will."

We lay there until a song comes on that describes exactly how I feel about being here.

"Come on." I stand up and move the blankets out of the way.

"What are you doing?"

"I want to dance with you to this song. Every time it comes on, I think of you." I pull her to me, and we start dancing right there in the back of the pickup truck. The light from the sun is long gone and the moonlight and stars surround us.

"You're so beautiful," I whisper as I stare at the woman who has become my entire world.

Kayla is everything I was looking for and many things I wasn't because I didn't know what I wanted or needed. She gets along great with my friends and family. Her parents seem to like me and visit regularly. Her mom even pulled me aside the other day and said to be prepared when we start having kids, they would be out once a week for family dinners. Kayla told me later that her father invested in his own helicopter so they can visit us more easily.

I ask her why he wouldn't just use hers. She smiled, saying he wanted a new play toy. A several million dollar play toy, apparently. Their lifestyle is still something I'm getting used to. Other than some name brand clothing, and the helicopter, Kayla is a pretty normal person. She doesn't flash her money and I almost forget she is a billionaire in her own right until she does something like buying a helicopter, or a champion racehorse because, and I quote, "it was too pretty to be racing around a racetrack."

The soft light on her face along with the smile she has for me lets me know this is the best time to tell her how I feel. I was waiting for the perfect moment, and I know this is it. Spinning her around to face me again, I get on one knee. The moment she sees me, she gasps. Then I pull the ring from my pocket and take a deep breath.

"I knew the moment Jason laid you on my exam table you were someone special. You're so full of life and have such a good heart. I loved watching you learn to fit in here in Rock Springs. And today you'd never know you weren't born here until you go do something like building a helicopter pad in the middle of a cow field."

She giggles at that, making me smile too.

"There was a time I didn't think we would be able to be here today to work this out. The mountain we had to climb seemed too much. But I know now it was too much because we were trying to do it on our own instead of together. I want to climb every mountain with you at my side. Will you marry me?"

When I open the box holding the ring, she gasps, falling to her knees.

"How did you afford this? It's so beautiful."

"Well, I asked your dad for your hand, but I also talked to Walter. He kept me hostage for three hours before giving me his blessing and then gave me this ring. It was the one he gave his wife on their thirtieth wedding anniversary. When he told me he wanted you to wear it, I thought it would be better than a store bought ring."

"You asked Walter?" She looks up at me with tears in her eyes.

"Yeah, I did. I need an answer, City Girl."

"Yes. Of course, I'll marry you. Yes!"

When I slide the ring on her finger, it's a perfect fit. She throws herself into my arms and I hold her right there on my knees in the bed of my truck.

She pulls back to stare at her ring again. "This is perfect, Brice. It means so much more than anything you could have bought. The size doesn't matter to me, it's the story behind it."

But the diamonds are not small, either. Walter's said it was upwards of four carats on the main stone and two more carats on the surrounding smaller stones. Not wanting to be apart one moment longer, I pull her into my lap, holding her tight as she moves the ring in the moonlight.

"You will have to ask Walter for the full story. But he said after he made a few money making advertising campaigns, he took her to the store for their anniversary and told her to pick out anything she wanted. He hadn't told her yet about the big payday he had. She picked out a much smaller version of this ring and he bought her this one with the biggest stone they had at the time. All the way home, she cried."

"I love that story."

"He has photos to go with it." I smile, and when she looks up at me again, those tears are still there in her eyes, but she looks so damn beautiful. I kiss her, a gentle kiss that turns heated fast.

I'm still in shock that I get to spend the rest of my life with her doing just this.

Epilogue
Kayla

One Year Later

We are at Sage's summer kick-off BBQ. Not that
we need a reason to get together and celebrate,
but it's nice to have a day to relax and catch up.
There are new babies getting passed all around
and the men are watching the older kids so the
women can sit in the sun and relax.

The last year has been a whirlwind. We got
married here in Rock Springs, and it was a sight
to be seen, for sure. Dallas socialite community
on one side of the church, Texas cowboys on
the other, and the two did not intermingle
the entire day. I'm not lying when I say the
whole town came out for the wedding, too. The
church was so packed, people were standing
outside. Because of the size of our wedding, we
took up the carnival grounds across from the
church for the reception. It was the only place
in town big enough to hold everyone.

I had a kick ass wedding planner, who made
the tents feel fancy with twinkle lights, and
decorations which I swear made an intimate

ambiance, and we felt like we were in some fancy romantic movie. Brice just wanted to get married and he didn't care about the details--typical man. But even he had a huge smile on his face all day. Though we weren't the only wedding in town that month.

Walter and Mrs. Willow got married, too. Though the wedding was much smaller. Those two then went to Vegas for a honeymoon and they can't get their story straight on what happened. All I know is, I haven't seen Walter happier. He finished his biography and with my help, got a contract on it, so he and Mrs. Willow are on a book tour right now and loving every minute of travel.

Mrs. Willow was hesitant to leave her grandkids, Anna Mae, and Jesse. But when Jesse met Natalie and moved to Walker Lake, Anna Mae was able to talk her into going. Brice and I are the latest people to buy a cabin on the lake in Walker Lake and I can tell you, it's the most relaxing place in the world.

Since buying our cabin, I've become friends with Sky and Jenna, who are Sarah's friends. They're in Rock Springs all the time for get-togethers. In fact, they are here now.

"So, Sky, what's new with you?" Sarah asks, but her tone suggests she knows what's new and is just trying to get Sky to admit it.

Those two have been friends since they were kids, and it shows. Mac says if it wasn't for Sky, they wouldn't be together, but I think there is more to it than that.

"Nothing much, was just in Walker Lake, visiting my parents," she says, shrugging her shoulders.

Sarah looks at Jenna, and they share a look.

"What are your plans after you leave here? Heading back to work in Dallas?" Jenna asks.

Sky hesitates for a moment before she sighs. "I guess we'll see. What about you Jenna? Rumors are flying that you have a boyfriend, but no one has any clue who it is."

Jenna blushes just enough to let us know it's true, but she doesn't say anything. Sarah told me she's writing a book and her parents are not only supportive, but rich, so she is living at home, in a house on the lake. Though she's working at the local diner for character inspiration and to make some spending money. It's how she and Sarah met, working together for a bit.

"Rumors are flying back home. You know how it is. If you look at someone too long, next thing you know everyone in town thinks you're getting married." Jenna tries to brush it off.

Sarah and I look at each other and it's clear from her expressions that she doesn't believe this any more than I do.

"Fine, don't tell me. I'll find out anyway, and the more you hide it, the worse it will be. Kayla, would you like to come with me to get a drink?"

Knowing she means Sage's special wine slushy mix, I don't hesitate to join her.

"Yes, I would." I stand up and we link arms.

Sky starts to stand. "Hey, I want a drink, too."

"Nope, drinks are for my friends that don't lie to me." Sarah says, dragging me into the house with Sky and Jenna protesting behind us.

"So, what are your theories with them?" I ask Sarah.

"Well, something is going on with Sky's job. I know she was working for a start-up in Dallas, and they have been downsizing, but I haven't seen any news on them. But there is definitely a guy involved. I'm not sure who. As for Jenna, if she isn't wanting to talk about the guy, it's because he doesn't like her back, or she isn't supposed to be dating him and doesn't want anyone to know. So that narrows things down."

"You two are just as bad as Riley and Lilly at matchmaking!" Sage says as she hands us our wine slushies.

"Well, if we knew who the guys were, then a little matchmaking wouldn't be a bad thing, now, would it?" Sarah asks.

"Nope, maybe a trip to my lake house and doing a little snooping couldn't hurt," I say.

Sarah smiles and looks out the kitchen window.

"That sounds like a great idea," she says, smiling. "That sounds like a really good idea."

• • • • •• • •• • •

Ready for Sky's story? Hers is a beauty and the beast retelling, a second chance. It is the start of the Walker Lake Texas Series in **The Cowboy and His Beauty**.

Learn all about Sage and her family, starting in **The Cowboy and His Runaway**.

Connect with Kaci M. Rose

Kaci M. Rose writes steamy small town cowboys. She also writes under Kaci Rose and there she writes wounded military heroes, giant mountain men, sexy rock stars, and even more there. Connect with her below!

Website

Facebook

Kaci Rose Reader's Facebook Group

Goodreads

Book Bub

Join Kaci M. Rose's VIP List (Newsletter)

More Books by Kaci M. Rose

Rock Springs Texas Series

The Cowboy and His Runaway – Blaze and Riley

The Cowboy and His Best Friend – Sage and Colt

The Cowboy and His Obsession – Megan and Hunter

The Cowboy and His Sweetheart – Jason and Ella

The Cowboy and His Secret – Mac and Sarah

Rock Springs Weddings Novella

Rock Springs Box Set 1-5 + Bonus Content

Cowboys of Rock Springs

The Cowboy and His Mistletoe Kiss – Lilly and Mike

The Cowboy and His Valentine – Maggie and Nick

The Cowboy and His Vegas Wedding – Royce and Anna

The Cowboy and His Angel – Abby and Greg

The Cowboy and His Christmas Rockstar – Savannah and Ford

The Cowboy and His Billionaire – Brice and Kayla

Walker Lake, Texas

The Cowboy and His Beauty - Sky and Dash

About Kaci M Rose

Kaci M Rose writes cowboy, hot and steamy cowboys set in all town anywhere you can find a cowboy.

She enjoys horseback riding and attending a rodeo where is always looking for inspiration.

Kaci grew on a small farm/ranch in Florida where they raised cattle and an orange grove. She learned to ride a four-wheeler instead of a bike (and to this day still can't ride a bike) and was driving a tractor before she could drive a car.

Kaci prefers the country to the city to this day and is working to buy her own slice of land in the next year or two!
Kaci M Rose is the Cowboy Romance alter ego of Author Kaci Rose.

See all of Kaci Rose's Books here.

Please Leave a Review!

I love to hear from my readers! Please **head over to your favorite store and leave a review** of what you thought of this book!

Made in the USA
Coppell, TX
06 June 2024